# Summer Heat:

## Beach Reads Volume One

## Authors:

Forbes Arnone

M.B. Feeney

R.E. Hargrave

*****

To Karen.
Enjoy!
MBFeeney

©2012

1

Summer Heat: Beach Reads Volume One

Summer Heat: Beach Reads Volume One

Published by
Renaissance Romance Publishing

**Copyright © Forbes Arnone 2013,
© M.B. Feeney 2013,
© R.E. Hargrave 2013**

The rights of Forbes Arnone, M.B. Feeney, and R.E. Hargrave to be identified as the authors of these work has been asserted by her under the ***Copyright Amendment (Moral Rights) Act 2000***

**License Notes**

Renaissance Romance Publishing
PO Box 22 Clarendon, TX 79226

Paperback ISBN-13: 978-0615834962
ISBN-10: 0615834965
Cover Art info: © Ben Goode | Dreamstime Stock Photos
Cover Design by: M.A. Richard

Summer Heat: Beach Reads Volume One

# Table of Contents

Summer Heat: Beach Reads Volume One

# In My Mother's Footsteps

By Forbes Arnone

# Acknowledgement:

I want to thank my husband for picking up the
slack while I follow my dreams, for taking
me to the beautiful island of Oahu for the first
time, and for the love and support that keeps
me going.
To my children, thank you for always believing
in me and loving me.
To my parents, all of you, thank you for always
supporting me.
I love you all.

# Chapter 1

## Knowledge

"Anela," Lennie Metting, our family attorney and longtime family friend, said as he tried to get my attention. "Anela, I need to know that you understand what I read you? Go through those papers soon, your graduation gift is in there. She left it with me not knowing if you'd want to see her, but wanting you to have it."

I nodded in reply.

Lennie and I were sitting in comfortable, dark brown, leather chairs next to the window in his office. The space had sleek lines and cold metals that looked as solemn as I felt. The beautiful view of the ocean and of Angel Island in the distance that spilled in through the grand window contrasted with both the décor and my mood. While tears streamed down my face, the beauty was lost on me. I sat in a complete daze and tried to process what the man sitting across from had said.

"Would you like some water?" he asked.

Shaking my head, I looked up and met his steel-gray eyes. They were kind and sympathetic. The recent death pained him, too. The beard on his face compensated for the lack of hair on the top of his head. His short stature did not reflect his character, as a fierce and passionate man. Lennie's reputation preceded him in court, but no one saw the kind man that my mother and I knew.

"No, thank you. I'm fine. Um . . . so is that all?" I tapped the file he'd given me after his speech.

"Yes, but I want you to call me if you need anything — and I do mean *anything*. You hear?" He started to stand.

I noticed how uncomfortable he appeared to be during the meeting, but he'd been very helpful nonetheless. In the last few weeks leading up to the meeting, he had assisted me in making the funeral arrangements and dealing with all of the legal paperwork that fell onto my shoulders.

Rising, I stuck out my hand for a formal shake, but instead Lennie pulled me into an embrace.

"Anela, please take care of yourself. Your mother would be very disappointed in me if I let anything happen to you, okay? And call me if you need anything."

"I understand, and thank you, Lennie." Pulling myself from his embrace took a great deal of strength. I longed for the feeling of a father's love and wanted to hold on to it for as long as I could, but I had to go. My mind needed sorting and there were plans to make.

As I made my way out of the office and back to my small cottage in Sausalito, California, I felt the panic come on. The list of things that I needed to do was surmounting and I felt overwhelmed.

Upon opening the door to the home I had shared with my mother since my birth, her scent hit me, just like it had every time I walked in here over the past two weeks. I wandered without cause around the small cottage before I plopped myself down on the couch. Everything in that house was old and artsy, just like the little town she lived in. My mother, Carla, had been an artist — a hippy even — and had fit so well with the other residents of Sausalito.

At twenty-two years old, I was about to graduate from Berkeley University in a week with a bachelor's degree in business management — for lack of a passion for anything else —. My graduation had been something my mother had been looking forward to seeing, but would never get to now. I'd been in my dorm room, studying for finals, when I received a phone call that my mother had passed away in our family home. She'd never been sick, so it hadn't made sense until the results of the autopsy were revealed. The coroner had concluded that Carla had had an aneurism that burst and drowned her brain. Research taught me about what an aneurism was and I found out that she must have been suffering from headaches and hadn't told anyone. Or maybe she had told someone, it just wasn't me. I hadn't been speaking to her at the time, after all.

It had always been just the two of us, since we didn't have any family left. She had a few friends around town, but none that I knew very well. With a shake of my head, I turned my attention to the list of things I needed to get done.

First thing on the list: I had to pack up my mother's belongings. The nagging urge to go through her stuff and find something sentimental kept bothering me. I needed to find a connection with my mother, even if I was angry with her. She'd left me all alone and I was livid about the lie I had been led to believe my whole life.

When I was about to start my senior year of college, Carla had sprung some life-changing and surprising news on me.

I'd come home for the summer and everything had been great. My love for running was a solitary thing, mainly because my mother refused to go with me. She always laughed that she was much too old and out of shape to start running. So, instead, I ran in the mornings while it was still brisk and in exchange, I'd let her teach me how to paint. In all honesty, I had zero talent and painted like a five year old, but she loved everything I'd created and told me she'd always cherish them.

During one of our sessions, I watched her paint the most beautiful scenery. A small chapel on the beach surrounded by billowing palm trees and lush plumeria trees. The colorful stained glass windows of the chapel reflected the sun and shot rays across the sand. When I asked her about it, she said it was her favorite place in the world. The whole scene blew me away and I felt myself being absorbed by its inviting nature. But when I asked her where it was, she replied with a single word: Ko'Olina. That had been all she gave me. I shrugged it off and didn't think too much about it.

Right before I left to head back to school, she sat me down — very formally — and began to tell me a tale.

*"Darling, listen to me. I have to tell you this before it kills me," she said with a blank face. She showed no emotion at all. It was like she had practiced it a million times, all so she could get through it without breaking down. "I know I told you that you didn't have a father and that I didn't know who he was. But I lied."*

*Her hands were working, steady and strong, to fold and unfold the pleat on her skirt.*

*"After I graduated high school, I took a vacation to Oahu, Hawaii. I spent a month there with my friends, just exploring the island and enjoying myself." While she spoke with strength, she didn't look at me. Instead, she watched her hands work on her skirt.*

*"It was a gift from my parents. They were old and didn't have the strength to take me anywhere themselves, so they sent me there with my two best friends at the time. Well, anyway, I met this soldier. He pursued me and*

*things just happened. We spent a lot of time together and I ditched my friends, which they never forgave me for," she said looking up at me for a moment.*

*"On my last night, we made love. He gave me his address and I went home, never looking back. Then, I found out I was pregnant with you."*

*Still looking me in the eyes, I could see her plea for understanding, but I couldn't give it to her, because I still didn't understand.*

*My heart began to beat in fury as if it had figured out the story before I did. I looked at my mother in such great confusion, knowing my eyes were pleading for a better explanation. Bitterness lodged itself inside me because the last thing I had allowed my mother to say to me had my world crashing down on me.*

*As my mother sat there telling me the tale of how she met her soldier and how I came to be, I couldn't believe my ears.*

*"So, he didn't die in battle somewhere? I mean you told me my father died before he could even meet me!"*

*"No, angel, he's very much alive. At least the last time I checked, he was."*

*Sitting there unable to move and listening in disbelief, my mouth had hung open in surprise and fury at her gall. I could not believe the words that were coming out of her mouth. It was all too much. My mother knew how much I had longed for a father, yet she failed to tell me I had one out there. How dared she?*

*Tingles swept through my body and I began to sway. My ears plugged and when I closed my eyes to steady myself, I saw stars. I could sense the signs of a faint coming on so I plopped myself back in the chair like a sack of potatoes, feeling defeated. Scooting my seat back, I shoved my head between my knees, most of all because I wanted to hide my face from my mother.*

*Then she spoke again.*

*"Anela, listen to me. I did what I thought was best. We had two different lives. I didn't want to be an Army wife and he wouldn't have left the military. He loved his job; it was his career. You know how old-fashioned Grandma and Grandpa were. They would have made me marry him. I didn't want that, so I refused to tell them. It just seemed easier."*

*I cut her off before she could say anything else. "Easier? Damn it, Mom. I would have had a father, for Christ's sake. Are you kidding me?"*

*The anger had built up and was ready to boil over.*

*"Anela, stop it! Things were more complicated back then. I shouldn't have even been with him before marriage and then I showed up from vacation pregnant by a man who had promised me nothing. He had plans for a career in the Army. I didn't want to ruin that for him. Once I made my decision, I was stuck*

*with it. And that was that. I'm sorry if you don't understand, but that's the way it is," she said.*

*I just stared at her in disbelief, shocked at all of the selfish words pouring out of her mouth.*

*"Look, darling, I'm sorry. I love you so much and I'm glad that I have you in my life." The tears rolled down her face, soaking her shirt.*

*I stood up in a flash and left.*

After that day, I ignored her phone calls, and never spoke to her again. I was consumed with bitterness over what she had denied me. I thought she was the most selfish person I had ever known.

Her sudden and unexpected death left me with such guilt and shame. I had shunned my mother for doing what she thought was best and it had cost me the last year of her life. My anger had made me a jerk and a spoiled brat. I hadn't deserved her love.

# Chapter 2

## Opportunity

My brown, wooden, antiquated cottage sat on top of a hill in Sausalito. The shingles were bleached out from exposure to the sun's rays. A beautiful, naturally-worn deck wound around the small chalet and gave me one of the best views in town. The bold, red peaks of the Golden Gate Bridge were visible through the light haze of fog over the ocean. With the hot sun working overtime to clear the sky, the fog always seemed to linger around the tops of the bridge. To my left, I could look down and see the rocky shore that the tourists often frequented. The slick brown and black seals liked to sunbathe on the boulders at the water's edge. People would gather to take pictures or have lunch in one of the quaint restaurants that overlooked the choppy, aqua-blue ocean.

I had grown up in Sausalito my entire life. With the exception of when I went to Berkley, I hadn't adventured into the city much. Sometimes, I'd take the ferry to Angel Island with my mountain bike and take leisurely rides or run the hills. I hadn't done that since I ran out of my mother's house, either.

Now that I had packed up all of her belongings — with the exception a few things I wanted to keep — I was exhausted. As I sat on the deck of my small cottage and stared out into the vast ocean, I felt anxious about the file that sat on my lap. Lennie had given it to me at his office three days before and I had yet to open it. The fear at what I'd find seeped in and turned my stomach.

Focusing my attention, I looked down at the folder and decided the time had come to face whatever was inside. My hands trembled as I lifted the two metal prongs and opened the flap. I tipped the folder upside down to empty the contents, finding the usual white sheets of paper that were full of legal jargon. How I wished I didn't know what they meant. Sifting through it all, I found a copy of the deed to the house, which stated that it had been transferred to my name. Also, there was the pink slip to my mother's car to be filled out and mailed to the Department of Motor Vehicles, and a small envelope with my mother's messy, artsy script on the front. One word had been written on it: Anela.

I took a deep breath and steeled myself for what new information might be in that letter. I pulled the paper out and began to read.

*To my dearest Anela,*

*I left instructions with Lennie to give you this letter only after one of us had* been able to share with you the truth about your father. After the way we left things, I wasn't sure if you'd want to see me at your graduation. Regardless, I plan on attending; I just hope you'll speak to me. I'm so proud of you, baby. You have to know that. I hope that one day you can forgive the deceit and lies, but at the time, I felt I made the right choice.

Enclosed is a round trip ticket to Oahu, Hawaii that Lennie arranged per my instructions for your graduation present. It's for a two-month stay at the Hilton Hawaiian Village in Waikiki. I believe you'll love it as much as I did.

So, if you permit me this one wish, I'd like you to go to Hawaii for two reasons. The first is so you can see all of my favorite sights from when I went there before I had you. I loved the island of Oahu so much. The feelings it evoked in me were as if I were one with the land itself.

The second reason is for you to try and find your father. I know that's what you want and I want you to be happy. I'm sorry if it took me too long and I kept that happiness from you. I really *thought that I could love you enough so that all you'd need was me.*

*Also, enclosed, is a list of everything I can remember of your father. I want you to know that I loved him, and that is why I gave myself to him, but I also want you to know why I had to let him go.*

*Have a wonderful vacation. I pray that you find your father and that he will love you as much as I do. Please forgive me.*

*I love you always my sweet girl, my little angel, my Anela.*


*Love,*
*Mom*


I stared in disbelief at the letter and then the list of items about my father. After so long, I couldn't believe I'd learned his name: Sergeant Neil McDonald. Tears pricked my eyes and my vision blurred. I swiped the moisture away with the sleeve of my sweater and scanned over other items on the list. Nothing else seemed important at that moment. When I opened the small envelope to slip the letter and list back in, I saw a small photograph. I pulled it out and tried to make sense of what I was seeing: a picture of my mother and *my father* sitting together on a big, red towel on the beach. It was an older photo, one from the seventies or eighties. It seemed faded or bleached out, but I could make out a few of his features.

Mom had long, black hair that had been pushed back with a headband and her skin appeared to be dark and tanned. My father — Neil McDonald — was also tanned and looked to have been fit and muscular. Just like me, he had blonde hair, but I couldn't tell the color of his eyes. Not that it mattered, because I knew I had my mother's cat-like, yellow eyes. Our driver's licenses listed them as green for color, but they were really several shades of yellow and gold, with maybe a speck of green. More than a few times, people had stopped us in mid-conversation after they'd seen the hue and gasped at the sight. They'd exclaim how unique and rare and beautiful our eyes were, but we knew most of them were trying to hide how strange they thought they were, too.

The excitement that came with finding that I had a piece of my father — something that said he was real — was overwhelming. We shared the same naturally champagne-color hair. I kept mine short on the sides and back, but long on the top so that it hung onto my forehead. My skin color was pretty fair at the moment, but I managed to tan pretty well. I just hadn't done that in a while, which led me to think about the upcoming vacation. Searching through the papers, I looked for the tickets and found an itinerary with a PNR — passenger name record — number. It was the first week of June; I had less than a month to get the legal stuff tied up, get a base tan, and buy some new clothes. At the thought of finding my father, I was overcome with a case of nerves.

San Francisco International was a nice-looking airport. The glass ceilings allowed light to flood the corridors and made them seem larger. I almost regretted taking the trip during such a busy time. The airport was packed with summer travelers and it was still early in the morning. Since I hadn't wanted to bother anyone with the chore of dropping me off at the airport, I used the Marin Shuttle Company. Not that there was anyone I *could* call; I didn't have many friends.

As I sat on the plane and waited for the rest of the passengers to get settled, I went through the itinerary I'd made for the trip. I had compared all of the places my mother wanted me to see and researched a few of my own, like the military base Schofield Barracks. A small car had been reserved for when I arrive so I could get around the island more easily. In the long run, it would be cheaper than paying for public transportation. At only twenty dollars a day, the car was a steal, in my opinion. In California, one wouldn't be able to rent a car for even close to that amount.

Even though I slept through most of it, the six-hour flight felt like an eternity. I read for a while and, of course, ate the sandwich I had packed for myself, knowing they didn't serve food on flights anymore.

"The fasten seatbelt sign has been turned on. Please buckle up as we prepare for landing. The local time in Oahu is ten-thirty a.m.," the flight attendant announced over the loud speaker.

My new adventure excited me and I had many things to look forward to. I just wished I had my mother here to share it with.

# Chapter 3

## Optimistic

Stepping off the airplane, the first thing that hit me was the thick, humid air. It was hot and sticky, but had such a sweet smell to it. The Honolulu International Airport had open walkways, lush greenery, and an array of colorful flowers that caught my attention everywhere my eyes roamed. Following all of the exit signs to the rental car transportation area, I found the bus that would take me to my car.

An hour and a half later, I was sitting behind the wheel of a brand new, bright yellow, convertible Volkswagen beetle. Looking in the rearview mirror at myself, I adjusted my sunglasses, and mussed up my bangs a bit with the tips of my fingers. I puckered my lips, and blew myself a kiss, before I popped the car into reverse, feeling quite giddy.

Using the map on my cellphone, it seemed like an easy drive: H-1 to Nimitz Highway to Ala Moana, and then to Kalia Road, where the hotel sat. The hotel was just as the brochure described: a village. Driving up to the valet, I noticed several small eateries, shops, and several different buildings that stood high in the sky.

Following the valet's directions into the lobby, I was surprised at the  sheer size of the room. The wooden check-in desk was the same length as an airline's ticket counter. I joined the queue and waited for my turn to receive my room information. Occupying myself with the décor of the lobby, I watched while people walked under the skylights and across the stone floor. The lobby was not fancy or lavish, more utilitarian. I was happy when it was my turn, and the process turned out to be painless.

With a map and key in hand, I made my way to the room, the path for which was simple to follow. There was a queen-sized bed, a small dining table, a desk and chair, and the bathroom. The room had more than I'd need for just myself. I put all of my belongings away and perused the room some more, noticing a small balcony that looked out onto the ocean. The hotel also had its own man-made pond for the kids to play in. Next to it was another building, this one with rainbow colors painted down the side.

Since it was already past noon and hunger had set in, I pulled out my list of things to do and decided to walk over to the International Market Place. Removing some unneeded things from my backpack, I grabbed my wallet and room key before setting out to explore.

While I walked, I felt something different. While I wasn't sure what it was, it felt good. I was happy and comfortable, not feeling at all odd for being on vacation alone. I blended in with the other tourists who were hustling and bustling around, and took in all of the scenery. Thin palm trees shot straight up into the sky and had smooth, brown bark, which led to a dozen grand, flapping leaves at the top. The ocean breeze made the trees look like tall, Hawaiian girls, dancing the hula. A small number of plumeria trees were scattered around, shocking and amazing me.

Back in California, the price for just one bald, six-inch branch was about forty-five dollars, yet here there was an overflowing abundance of them. Some had yellow or white flowers, while others had pink blossoms. Planted by each crosswalk were beautiful hibiscus bushes with red, purple, and bright yellow blooms. The scent of flowers, food, suntan lotion, and the ocean were all around me. I felt at home in a place that I'd never been before.

Once I arrived at the Market Place, I noticed there were even more people milling around. The entry way led to several rows of tables, each one with small thatched roofs. They sold anything and everything Hawaiian, like gorgeous jewelry made in the shape of plumerias or little barrels with one's name written on them in the native language. There were racks full of clothes, tables with novelty items like magnets and key chains, and a lot of food. My eyes locked in on a table with flavored coffee, chocolate-covered macadamia nuts, coconut macadamia nuts, and fresh slices of mango and pineapple. All of it had my mouth watering and my stomach rumbling so I decided to walk over to the Hard Rock Cafe and have a sandwich while going over my plans for the next day.

After a good night's sleep, I woke up with the intention of going to Schofield Barracks to inquire about my father. I had such mixed feelings on that issue and I wasn't sure if I really wanted him to be there or not. If he was, I worried that he wouldn't want me. And if he wasn't there? Well, that would be disappointing to say the least, and it meant that I might never get the chance to meet him. Hot and cold feelings alternated through me. For the past month, I had been a nervous wreck, but I vowed to think positive thoughts about the trip to the barracks. If I got nothing from inquiring there, then I'd head on over to the Dole Plantation.

Pulling up to the barracks felt strange. Since I had no idea where to go to ask my questions, I went with the obvious choice: The Information and Referral Service Office. It had been the only place with "information" in the title. As I strolled to the office door on Kolekole Avenue, I began to worry. What if they didn't want to give me any details? I'd brought the letter my mother left me and the picture of my parents together.

*Wow*, I thought, *parents — plural.*

Steeling my nerves, I opened the door and put on my brightest smile. A man about my age sat at a desk in ACU's —Army Combat Uniform — and was typing away on the computer.

When he lifted his head and looked at me, I stepped forward, held out my hand, and said, "Hello, my name is Anela Alborn and I need some information."

He shook my hand. "Yes, Ma'am, Private Takata. I hope I can help."

His teeth were so white that, when he smiled, they almost stole my attention away from the angry, red and purple, cystic acne sores on his face. He was of Asian decent with dark eyes and buzzed hair. It looked like he stood an inch or so shorter than me, and he seemed a little thin.

I began to weave my parents' tale and the secret that had been kept from me until recently. Private Takata was polite and listened until I finished, then he told me that he knew exactly who Neil McDonald. He explained that my father was now a Colonel, and he sort of laughed at the picture I showed him. When I looked at him questioningly, he shrugged.

"It's just weird seeing him so young," he said without apology.

"Oh," I answered and then my mind wandered to what he might look like now.

"Anyway, he's not here now," he added, and I sagged in defeat.

"Well, do you know when he'll be back?" I questioned, prepared to come back anytime.

He cocked his head back and looked at me. "It may be a couple of weeks to a month. His battalion just came back from Iraq and Colonel McDonald is on leave."

Takata shrugged again and I felt my face fall.

*A month.* I thought I'd have more time with him and now I had to wait a whole month.

"Is there any way I can leave a message or some way for you to contact me when he comes back?" I asked, desperation filling my voice. I wanted to leave my information and go before I started to cry, feeling more than disappointed with the recent developments.

Takata said I could do both so I gave him my information and a note for the Colonel and left. At first, I wasn't sure what to write, but then I just mentioned my mother's name and the need to speak with him about her. The Private promised he would pass on the message and call me when he got back from his trip.

Running out of the office, I almost knocked down another soldier on my way out. He grabbed me by the elbows to steady me.

"Excuse me, ma'am," he said.

I was so flustered and embarrassed that the tears began to flow. Squeaking out a quick "No, I'm sorry" I ran straight to the car without looking back.

I forgot about my plans to go to the pineapple plantation and went straight to the North Shore. There was a long stretch of beach and, after I found a parking space, I searched out a deserted spot and sat in the sand, watching the waves. I shouldn't have been so upset; I should have expected that tracking him down wasn't going to be easy, but the disappointment sat heavy in my stomach, weighing me down. Over the past month, my dream had been to find my father and have an instant relationship with him. I pictured him sweeping me off my feet and showering me with the fatherly love I had been without for the past twenty-two years.

I had been such a strong girl before my mother died. Now the fact that I was all alone in the world felt overwhelming. No one would know or even care if something happened to me. There wouldn't be anyone to mourn or miss me. Maybe Lennie would for a minute, but then he'd move on with his life and his family. Otherwise, there wasn't anyone.

I slipped my flip-flops off and walked the length of the small beach, close to the water. Walking in up to my knees, I spotted bubbles and small ripples in several places. With closer inspection, I noticed they were coming from huge turtles. Each one was about the size of the circle my arms would make if I held my hands together and bowed out my elbows. On the plus side, they didn't seem afraid of me. I was amazed at being so close to nature in that way. Turtles weren't common in the ocean around San Francisco; at least I'd never seen them there. But here, there were tons of them and I noticed they swam alone. Just like me, surrounded by tons of people but all alone.

# Chapter 4

## Breathtaking

The next morning, I found myself feeling a bit depressed when I woke up. Since I couldn't see my father, I felt the need to start on my mother's to-do list. My goal was to find some waterfalls that she suggested I check out. I drove for over an hour in the direction I'd found on the Internet but still couldn't find them. Somehow, I ended up in a small parking lot, facing a dead end that looked like it was behind a remote hotel. I figured I could find someone and ask for directions, but when I pulled into the parking lot, I saw a small beach tucked away from the street's view. Without hesitation, I parked the car, climbed out, and ran over to see if it I could hang out there.

Tall, reflective buildings sat to the right, with their name in grand letters: J.W. Marriott, Ko'Olina. Right in front of me, was a small manmade beach. A walkway lined the length of the beach, leading to a beautiful chapel on the left at which I gasped. That was the chapel my mother had painted. It clicked in an instant. The stained glass windows, the billowing palm trees, and the small beach that surrounded it was a complete replica. At first, it almost felt like déjà vu. The amazing details my mother had been able to depict in her painting awed me.

The name of the beach sparked the memory of the conversation I'd had with her while she painted that beautiful picture.

*We sat side-by-side with our easels in front of us, facing a window with a gorgeous ocean view. Carla told me to paint what I saw, and as literal as I was, I began painting the view before me. When I peaked at her canvas, I saw that it was of a beautiful chapel. It looked so small compared to the vast beach surrounding it and the tall palm trees that appeared to sway above the church's steeple. My mother had every detail of the stained glass windows done to perfection, and there were trees surrounding the building.*

*"Mom, what are you painting? I thought we were supposed to paint what we see," I asked, very confused.*

*"I am, honey. I'm painting what my mind's eye sees. It's a place I've been to before and I thought it so beautiful that I took a mental picture of it, keeping it with me forever," she explained with a sigh. She seemed so wistful, regretful over something that had to do with that church.*

*"I like it a lot, Mom, but what kind of trees are those?" I pointed to the semi-tall trees with a lot of branches shooting out in all directions. Each one was filled with blooms of little white flowers with a touch of yellow in the middle. They were magnificent and so different than anything I had ever seen.*

"Those, my dear, are plumeria trees. The scent from those little flowers is so sweet and pungent."

"Wow, they sound as good as they look. So, where did you see that chapel?" I asked.

Her eyes zoned out even more than they were while she was painting, and she answered, "Ko'Olina."

That was it. With the flourish of her paintbrush, I knew the conversation was over.

My eyes followed the path all the way to the hotel, which sat on the right. Next to the small strip of walkway, lay a patch of grass littered with palm trees for shade and then the sand led to the water. Up and down the small beach, local families were lounging. Well, they seemed like locals. They didn't look like the typical tourists: super white skin, dazed expression, always in awe, and crazy clothes — you know, like things they only wear to go on vacation. No, these people were dark, bigger, and wore everyday clothes, things people wear when they're home: worn out shorts, shirts, and flip-flops. They had barbecues and floating toys for their kids. The adults lay under the trees on the grass, while some of the kids played in the sand making castles and others splashed in the water.

One more look at the beach and I knew I felt the same as my mother had: enchanted. That was where I wanted to be, so I ran back to the car and grabbed my belongings. That secluded little beach called to me and made me feel like I'd discovered a secret. Prepared for an outing around water, I already had my bathing suit on, a lunch packed, and a couple of towels. When I returned to the entrance of the beach, I began to scope a place to camp out. I preferred the grassy area but the whole stretch seemed full, except for a small area just to my left. With a shrug, I strolled over and placed my belongings under the single palm tree. It gave very little shade, but I wanted to feel the sun and I had enough sun block to get me through my transition from pale to bronze.

I had never felt better while I relaxed and enjoyed my day. The sun felt wonderful as I lay on my stomach and devoured one of the latest sexy Scottish Highlander books that I'd become addicted to reading. Looking up from my book, I noticed a group of rowdy guys setting up a volleyball net. Then, I noticed them dropping a pile of towels and T-shirts beside me.

*Great!* I thought with sarcasm.

Sitting up to lean against the tree, my eyes scanned the group and I noticed there were about twenty men — all soldiers. Their crew cuts, dog tags, and muscled bodies gave that much away. When I turned to look around at the locals, I noticed their scowling faces and heard a few that were close to me call them "*haoles*." It was obvious they didn't like the soldiers or want them on their beach.

The sudden volleyball game became more interesting than my book. Yeah, men in kilts were sexy, but so were soldiers in shorts and nothing else. It took no time at all before they were sweating and taking turns playing. While some of them played, others sat down or went for a quick swim. A few came toward the pile of towels next to me and I recognized Private Takata from the information office the day before. I turned my head, not wanting to be noticed, but it was too late. Our eyes met and I saw the smile on his face grow. I groaned a bit. My relaxing day had vanished.

"Hey, I know you. You came by the office yesterday," he exclaimed.

"How are you today, Private Takata?"

He plopped down next to me and fished out his towel and blotted the sweat off his face.

"I'm good, thanks. Nice to have a day off," he said.

"Hm-hmm," I murmured in response.

"Dragon, throw me my towel. It's the blue one," a handsome man yelled, coming toward us. His crystal-blue eyes shined in contrast to his dark, black hair. He stood a few feet in front of me, but I could tell he was as tall as my five feet, nine inch stature. His thin, almost lanky body was filled with defined muscles. As he got closer, I noticed his eyes were like the petals of pale, blue forget-me-nots. There was no smile on his thin, long face, but it wasn't harsh, either.

I looked at Takata, laughing as I questioned, "Dragon?"

"He sees dragons," the other man replied in a serious tone and expression.

*He's messing with me! He has to be,* I thought. My right eyebrow arched and I crooked my head expecting more of an explanation.

"Tell her," crystal-eyes urged with a wave and chin jerk toward me.

Takata turned bright red and stared at crystal-eyes with a look of hope that perhaps he'd let him off the hook, but no. Crystal-eyes just raised an eyebrow to show his seriousness and Takata turned his head toward me.

With a shrug, he sat up straighter and in a determined manner began his theory. "Well, ma'am —"

I cut him off. "You can call me Anela."

The ma'am stuff was getting old and I wanted him to knock it off.

He smiled, flushing red again.

"Well, Anela, you see, we all have dragons. Some of us see them and some don't, but I see mine. Each dragon has a strength that he gives his human and mine is intelligence." Takata pointed to his temple. Then, with the most serious tone I had ever heard, he continued to explain his theory. "Have you seen your dragon?"

Able to mask my feelings, I kept my face blank. I didn't want them to see the confused and dumbfounded expression I desired to let loose. Looking around and waiting for people to jump out with cameras, I had a feeling I was being punked. When I snapped out of it and realized no one was there with cameras, I turned back at the friend, in order to gauge his expression. He seemed dead serious. Looking back at dragon-boy, I couldn't hold back my thoughts any longer.

"Are you guys messing with me?" My tone was strong and accusatory.

"No, m — Anela, I'm serious. Look." Takata stood up and began doing slow martial arts moves, lifting one leg and then swirling his hand around. This went on for about five minutes, and he attracted the attention of some of the other soldiers.

"Yo! Is your dragon speaking to you again?" one of the guys by the volleyball net yelled.

"Go, Dragon! Go, Dragon! Go, Dragon!" another of the soldiers sang.

I was in Crazy Town, because one of the other guys came running over, and started jumping around in a very strange and excited manner.

"Yeah, Dragon. I see mine. I've told you, right? He's big, red, and scaly with long talons." He was teasing Takata.

I shook my head.

Dragon stopped his moves and looked at me. "See, that was my dragon speaking to me through movements. That's how he can give me the words to explain everything to you. All of our dragons communicate with us in different ways. You might not know how your dragon speaks to you yet, but you will one day," he said, ignoring everyone else.

*O...kay?*

My head was swimming with all of the craziness. I had a feeling he was unstable and wondered how he could be in the military, but it made me angry that they teased him over his theory. Even though I did find it a bit odd and funny, I just didn't want to condone that sort of treatment and wanted to make him feel better.

"Takata, I'll have to look out for my dragon, then. Thank you so much for telling me about it," I told him, trying on the most sincere smile I could summon.

# Chapter 5

# Challenge

The book I was reading was calling to me, so I picked it back up.

"Come on, dragon, you're up." A shout came from the volleyball net.

Takata jumped up and ran to the net, yelling that he'd see me around over his shoulder.

Crystal-eyes strolled closer to me and took Takata's place. I had a bit of anger still bubbling inside me from this guy calling him out like that.

"Did you have to do that in front of everyone?" I groused.

His head snapped at me as if I had no right to question him. "Do what?"

I gave him the bitch-brow and scoffed. "You know what. Embarrassing him like that in front of everyone. That was fucked up!"

"You have no idea what you're talking about," he spat.

We fell silent. I wanted to pick up my book and read some more; but I couldn't concentrate on the words. I was too busy wondering what he had meant. What possible explanation could he have for doing that to one of his friends?

Takata was running toward us again. "Hey, Sivers, you know this is the girl that ran into you yesterday at the office. She was in there looking for Colonel McDonald — her father."

Dragon had a case of verbal vomit. He'd just laid my business out there for this asshole to hear. I felt the need to explain but before I could say anything, Sivers turned and questioned me.

"He's on leave. If you're his daughter, shouldn't you have known that?"

"Well, I was going to say that I don't know him yet. I just found out he's my father, and I came to meet him. Not that it's any business of yours." The annoyance in my voice was noticed and he blanched at my tone. *Whatever!*

I went back to my book, hoping he'd get the hint that I didn't want to talk to him any longer. Luck was on my side for a while when they all went back to the game and left me alone. The highlander in my book had to find his kidnapped wife and then kill all of her abductors. I sighed; he was so dreamy! For once in my life, I wished that I had a love interest as dedicated and sweet to me as this highlander was to his wife. I'd never had a real boyfriend. Well, I had dated, but it was always disappointing and either I never felt a connection or didn't like the guy's self-centered attitudes. It seemed like they all wanted a woman to take care of them without getting anything in return. What woman would want that? Not me. I wanted someone who'd love me with every ounce of his heart and soul.

Someone who wanted to take care of me and in return, I'd love him just as much and give him the world.

"What are you reading?"

I looked over and saw Sivers sitting there again. His eyes were distracting because they were so light — an icy blue with a line of dark blue around them.

"Nothing you'd enjoy, I'm sure. It's a romance novel about a Scottish highlander," I muttered, and my voice dripped sarcasm.

He laughed at me — a sinister laugh. "You think I can't appreciate romance in general or just a romance novel?"

I shrugged. "Both."

Sivers sat down next to me, with his knees up, feet planted in the sand, and his hands hanging over his legs and shook his head at my comment. "Wow, you're pretty judgmental."

Not wanting to go back and forth with this guy, I just ignored him.

"So, how long are you here for?" he asked when I didn't answer.

A loud, exasperated breath left me, and I emphasized it by pulling my body up and down. I supposed he didn't get the hint that I didn't want to talk to him — and didn't even like him, for that matter.

"I'll be here for two months," I grumbled, not elaborating.

"Hmm —"

"Sivers, you're up!" one of the other guys called out.

He jumped and didn't even try to finish his last thought, for which I was thankful.

Without too many more disruptions, I was able to finish reading and eat my lunch. There was a bit of small talk with a few of the guys that came for their towels, but other than that, neither Sivers nor Takata sat down with me again.

It was starting to get late and I wanted to be back at the hotel for dinner, so I began packing my belongings. I looked around to see if anyone noticed but they all seemed involved in their game, so I made my way back to my car. Just when I reached the parking lot, I heard someone calling out to me.

"Hey, wait! Hold on!"

Looking around to see who was yelling, I saw Sivers running toward me. I stopped with some reluctance, but it occurred to me that I may have left something behind. As he ran to me, I couldn't deny that he was an attractive man, yet when he opened his mouth it was a complete turn off. Sometimes the person who may not be very attractive on the outside becomes so once they are able to show their personality and have an intelligent conversation. Then again, with most handsome guys that most women swooned over, it all came crashing down with their self-centered attitudes. This didn't apply to *all* men, of course, but it just went to show not to judge a book by its cover.

"You're leaving?" he asked when he caught up to me.

I noticed he was just a few inches taller than me, just like I had predicted.

"Umm, yeah. It's getting late."

"Oh. I was going to ask you if I could take you to dinner tonight." He spoke with some apprehension.

I felt my eyes bulge out of my head. Was I misreading his signals earlier? I thought he was uninterested and a tad rude.

"Well, if you really want to. I mean, I'm just surprised."

He cocked his head and looked surprised. "I'd like that very much."

We exchanged information and I went back to my hotel, trying to figure how I felt about going out alone with this guy, whose first name I didn't even know.

# Chapter 6

# Confidence

A short nap and soak in the tub had me feeling refreshed for my dinner date with Sivers. It felt strange that I didn't even know his first name and I wondered if he knew mine. I assumed that he'd probably ask Takata.

My long, lean legs were hidden under a white, flowing skirt and my thin torso was covered with an orange tank top. I draped a silver-linked belt over my ample hips, added some silver bangles on my left wrist, and put on a pair of orange, flat sandals. Then, I slicked my hair back off my face and put on a little eye makeup and lip-gloss. Since my skin had gotten some color, I didn't need any blush.

Sivers was supposed to meet me in front of the main lobby at seven o'clock and I was beginning to get nervous. There were so many thoughts flooding my mind. A romance was not something I wanted, or had even anticipated when I made plans to come to Hawaii. I didn't want to tumble into the same trap that my mother had and fall for a soldier who might not want a serious relationship. I figured I'd just see how it went and take it from there.

I made my way down to the lobby and found Sivers standing tall and confident. He spotted me and a real smile spread across his face; it surprised me, as it was the first time I'd seen one on his face. Closing the distance between us, I felt shy all of a sudden.

"Hi," I murmured.

"Hi. You ready?" he asked.

With a nod, I walked out of the hotel's village with him.

The restaurant he chose was a few blocks away. We took an elevator up to the top floor of the building and stepped into a lobby. It had plush, red carpet and a beautiful picture of Diamond Head on the wall with the "Top of Waikiki" written above it. The hostess walked us into the dining room and I realized we were in one of those revolving restaurants. We were seated right next to a window and the night was beautiful. The sky had been lit up in gorgeous streaks of pink, purple, and orange as the sun set behind Diamond Head. Tears pricked my eyes from the sight before me. Emotion hit me as I realized I'd never be able to share this night with my mother or described the sunset to her ever — or apologize for my behavior.

I turned to Sivers and said, "Thank you for bringing me here. It's so beautiful"."

He graced me with another dazzling smile. "You're welcome."

"You know, I don't even know your first name."

"Christian — Christian Sivers," he replied.

I grinned before asking, "Do you know mine?"

The tips of his ears were bright red. "I do. I asked Takata."

Smirking, I leaned back in my seat. "I figured you would."

I ordered a glass of white wine while Christian ordered a beer. We continued to talk until the waitress approached to take our order. While I sipped my wine, I noticed Christian seemed calm. He sat back in his chair, calm without a worry in the world, while I sat forward, nervous and fidgeting. So not fair. And boy, did he look handsome. The paisley, short-sleeved button down shirt he was wearing in different shades of blue complimented his eyes. I thought he was quite handsome.

"Have you decided?" Christian queried.

I nodded. "I'll have the Green Tea Smoked Salmon, please," I told the waitress, pointing to the item on the menu.

"Great choice." She beamed and turned to Christian. "And for you, sir."

"I'll have the Beef Wellington."

"Great. I'll have that out shortly. Let me know if you need anything in the meantime."

"Thank you," Sivers replied.

"Thanks," I said.

There was an awkward block of silence and I decided to break it.

"How long have you been in the Army?" Christian met my gaze for the first time and gasped. I ducked my head, letting my eyelids flutter to a close. He reached across the table, placed his forefinger under my chin to lift up my face, and looked at me again.

"You have the most beautiful eyes I have ever seen," he murmured, enunciating every word.

I closed my eyes again in disbelief. People were always so mystified by my eyes and usually not in a good way. I was teased quite a lot as a kid due to the unique color of my irises. The kids had been cruel and relentless; they would meow at me and tell me I was part cat. Even though I knew it wasn't true, it still stuck with me and scarred me. It was difficult to adjust to the reactions I had been getting as an adult. Most adults said they liked my eyes and that it was a good thing to have them resemble the eyes of a cat, but feeling so self-conscious about it was just a hard habit to break.

He dropped his hand from my face, picked up his beer, and took a sip. "Please don't shut me out. It's just that I have never seen eyes that color before. They're like cat eyes."

"I think you have beautiful eyes, too. In fact, I admired them all day. I've never seen eyes that color blue before," I told him.

Christian laughed before giving me his sexy, cocky smile, the one where just one side of his mouth lifted up and it screamed, "*Yeah, I know I'm fine.*"

I just shook my head at him.

"So, my question?" I prompted.

"Oh, yeah. Ten years. I enlisted right out of high school."

Picking up my glass, I sipped my wine. "So, have you been to Afghanistan?"

"No, my battalion went to Iraq. I've done three tours so far, but I think the most recent one we did will be the last," Christian answered.

"Oh, I see." Sitting back, I thought of how going away to war might have affected him. Pictures of death and devastation flashed through my mind and I wondered what it had really been like for them and not what we saw on television. I didn't ask though, because I felt that was a sensitive subject.

"So what brings you here to Hawaii?" he inquired.

I looked down at the table and began fidgeting with the fork. The table was set with a plain, white tablecloth and maroon napkins. A small, votive candle gave us a bit of light as it reflected off its crystal holder.

"Well, it's a long story," I stated, waving my hand in front of me like I was clearing the air.

Christian reached over and held my hand. "We have time if you want to tell me. I'd like to get to know you better."

I looked at his hand covering mine, surprised to see his nails were manicured. He had pretty fingers that were a perfect length for his hand.

"Let's see. My mother died about a month and a half ago from an aneurism. I hadn't spoken to her — not a single word — for ten months before she passed. The summer before, she told me that I did, in fact, have a father after twenty-two years of thinking I didn't. But he knows nothing about me. She met him here in Hawaii and loved it here so much that she wanted to send me here to experience the island as she had all those years ago, even if it was without her. Also, it would serve as an opportunity to meet my father," I explained with a bit of sarcasm, but then regretted it instantly.

"So, the Colonel knows nothing about you?" It was clear that Christian was shocked, too.

"Nope. Not a thing," I retorted.

The waitress brought us our food and I decided to dig in with hopes of changing the subject.

"Can I get you two anything else?" our waitress asked.

"Just some more water when you have time, please." I gestured to my empty glass.

"Sure, be right back," she answered.

"Do you know him? The Colonel?" I couldn't help asking, apprehension lacing each word.

"Yes. We were in Iraq together the first time, but he's been promoted several times since then. He's our Brigade Commander now. He's a great guy."

I continued to eat, not wanting to hear how nice he was. It just dug the knife in deeper at how I'd missed not only having a father, but perhaps a good one, too.

## Chapter 7

## *Appreciate*

The salmon tasted delicious and I enjoyed the company. With his hair cut close to his head, a slightly crooked nose, and laugh lines around his mouth, Christian was a handsome man. The few times he had smiled were quite a treat. He didn't show many teeth, but the side of his mouth would lift in a seductive smirk. It was alluring and attractive, but my gaze continued to go back to his almond-shaped eyes. The longer I looked at them, the more I noticed how dusky they were, with dark lashes that outlined them almost like eyeliner. I hadn't figured him out yet. He was hard to read. His serious, straight-to-the-point demeanor was disconcerting and confusing. Was he nervous and just knew how to hide it well? Or did he not care enough to be nervous?

Christian watched me as he put a piece of steak into his mouth, and I did the same as I took bites of my salmon. The few dates I had been on were strange. I never liked the feeling of being pursued, to the point where it felt like stalking. Christian was aloof but not too much. I enjoyed it so far, but also liked the thought of being loved by a man. Yeah, I was digging deep there. I had never been loved by a man — not by a father or boyfriend — and thought it made me a tad pathetic.

"Anela?"

I looked up at Christian, surprised that he was talking to me and I hadn't heard any of it.

"I'm sorry. I just got lost in my thoughts," I mumbled.

He laughed at me, but I was getting used to him thinking I was funny all the time. "That's okay. What were you thinking about?"

"What it would be like to have a father," I fibbed.

The waitress arrived and Christian switched his attention to her. I was grateful for the save.

"Would you like dessert?" he asked.

I wiped my mouth with my napkin and placed it back on my lap. "Um, no, thank you. I'm stuffed. Do you?"

"I'm good."

When the check arrived, I offered to help pay, only to be reprimanded for even suggesting that I contribute. We left, opting to go for a stroll around the market place. The streets looked so different at night. My night vision wasn't great, but the dark streets were backlit by restaurants and nightclubs. During the day, the people that milled around were dressed mostly in street clothes, but at night, everyone looked more put together. The women were wearing all forms of fancy wear, their makeup and hair perfected, and the men were freshly shaven with nice slacks and short-sleeved dress shirts.

There was also a diverse type of crowd. Instead of families and older people, the streets were filled with young people who were closer to my age. Christian and I were walking side by side when — to my surprise — he reached for my hand and held it. His fingers felt warm, natural, and comfortable wrapped around mine. However, with the whole last-minute date thing and along with the handholding, I realized I hardly knew anything about him. What if he had a wife or girlfriend?

"So, where are you from originally?" I asked, trying to ease my way into the heavy stuff.

"I'm from a small town in New Mexico. You?"

Okay, short answer.

"Oh, that's nice. I'm from a small town near San Francisco. So, is all of your family still there?" I was trying to squeeze out information little by little.

"Yes. My mom and dad own a restaurant that they operate together. My older brother and sister also live there with their families, too. Natasha and her husband have a ten-year-old daughter, Alissa. Joseph and his wife have four kids. They're crazy, because those kids are all under ten. My sister in law just pumped them out one after the other." He laughed, shaking his head. "We're all really close and the kids are all adorable. It's a nice, quaint little town."

We were walking at a slow pace, taking in the sites and giving us time to have a conversation which I was thankful for.

Christian looked over at me. "And you? You don't have any family left back home?"

I shook my head. "No, I don't. My grandparents passed away when I was little. My mother was a late-in-life baby. I think my grandmother was in her late forties when my mother was born," I said, feeling sorry for myself.

"But now you'll be able to meet your father."

"I suppose so. I just want him to know I exist. More than anything I'd love for him to instantly accept and love me. But there's no guarantee that he will and that scares the shit out of me." I shivered at the thought of my father rejecting me.

Christian shrugged. "I don't see why he wouldn't. He's married, but I don't think he has any other kids."

"And you? Do you have a wife or kids? Maybe a girlfriend somewhere," I blurted out, wishing I had filtered that last bit. Now it was my turn to shrug. "I'm sorry. I didn't mean for it to sound intrusive or anything. But it's something that's been on my mind."

I could see his chest shaking and feel his hand jerking around mine. As usual, he was laughing at me.

"You get a kick out of laughing at my expense, don't you? It seems that's all you do,"

I huffed, teasing him and trying to act upset by his behavior.

"To answer all of your questions: no. I don't laugh at your expense. I just love your ability to say what's on your mind." Christian smiled. "No, I'm not married, nor do I have a girlfriend or kids. How about you? Since you asked me, I think it's something I should know, too."

"No. I've never even had a boyfriend," I answered.

Somehow while we were getting to know each other, we arrived in front of my hotel. He walked me back to our meeting point and the shyness crept in again, unsure what all this meant to him and what he would expect from me.

"Thank you so much for a wonderful dinner and great company. I enjoyed myself," I murmured.

We were standing to the side of the lobby in a small grassy area. Facing each other, he reached out to hold both of my hands with his and leaned in to kiss me — or so I thought. Instead, he moved his hands up to cup my face and looked deep into my eyes.

"It was my pleasure, Anela. Thank you for giving me a chance tonight." Christian kissed me on the forehead, lingering there for a few moments before stepping back. "You have my number and I have yours, so I'll call you tomorrow. I have to work this week, but then I'm on vacation. I'm not going home this time. Maybe we can spend more time together."

"I'd like that. Good night."

And then I turned to walk up to my room.

The next day brought out some strange feelings from inside of me. I enjoyed my night with Christian, but wasn't sure how to proceed with him. My greatest fear would be falling into the same predicament my mother had found herself facing but did I want to give up a chance for love?

*Hmph!* Look at me, getting ahead of myself. I didn't even know if he liked me as more than a friend. Frustrated with myself and the feelings flowing through me, I decided to go for a run down by the beach.

The concierge told me about a great route for advanced runners right outside the hotel that would take me to Diamond Head Volcano. The Hawaiian name for the volcano is Lēʻahi. In translation, lea means brown ridge; the second part of the name, ahi, stands for and resembles an ahi tuna when looking at the volcano from afar. It was dormant and not expected to erupt again. Since it was on my list of things to see, I wanted to climb up there. The route was difficult because some of it was sand and other parts road, but it was the elevation that really kicked my ass. It had been over a month since I had run and I was used to running the Sausalito hills, not up the side of a volcano. Also, the weather here was different. The heat was thick and very humid, but I liked the challenge. I pushed myself through all eight miles, working out every single disappointment and new challenge that came my way. Because I was too caught up in my own head, I barely paid attention to the scenery. I'd come to the decision to just let things happen the way they were meant to be. I wouldn't push or force anything with Christian and just go with the flow.

After some necessary stretching exercises and a refreshing shower, I decided to drive to the North Shore again. I packed all of my necessities for the day and noticed I had two missed calls and one message on my voicemail. The calls were from Christian and I assumed the message was, too. I pushed my voicemail button, hearing his voice trickling through the speaker a moment later.

"Anela, hi. Um, I just had a quick break and wanted to check in and say hello. Okay, well, I have to get back. Maybe you can return my call. All right, then. Bye."

*Oh my goodness!* He sounded strange and unsure, which seemed very unlike him. I decided to call him before I left to see what he wanted. I moved out to the tiny balcony overlooking the ocean and waited for him to answer. After several rings, I was about to end the call when he picked up.

"Hello?" he answered, sounding out of breath

"Christian, hi. It's Anela, returning your call."

"Oh, good you got my message. Hold on a second." I heard some rustling before he started speaking again.

"Okay, sorry about that. We were doing drills and it's been pretty intense. So, did you have any plans today?"

"Oh, well, I was about to drive to the North Shore for some lunch at this shrimp truck I heard about, Giovanni's, and that's it. I mean, I was just going to see stuff and keep myself busy." My nerves were making me ramble like a crazy woman.

"Well, I get off in an hour. If you'd like, I could join you. I'm sort of on your way. You can swing by and pick me up."

*Remember you said you wouldn't fight it. Just go with the flow,* I thought.

"Sure, that sounds great. Okay, well, where do I find you?"

"Just go to the information office you were at the other day. I'll meet you there in an hour and a half," he told me. "I've got to get back. See ya."

"Bye," I said, but he'd already hung up.

# Chapter 8

# Happiness

A bit overanxious, I left right away and ended up sitting in the parking lot for almost forty minutes before Christian arrived. I saw him walking toward my car with his typical, serious facial expression. My heart sped up at the sight of him and it confused me. Consciously, I didn't get excited looking at him, but with the way my body was reacting, I supposed I was happy. I had no idea what it meant or if I even had any feelings for him. Although, I did think he was very good looking, I still found him difficult to figure out. He walked to the passenger side of the car and opened the door. When he climbed in, I laughed at how his legs curled up in front of him because they were too long for the car. He pushed the seat back as far as it could go, giving himself more room.

Christian's lips curved into the special smirk I'd come to expect from him. "Hey."

I ducked my head, unsure why I felt wary. "Hi."

"Are you hungry? Because I'm starved."

"Yes, famished," I replied.

Christian gave me a few directions on how to get off the base, saying that they were short cuts.

"You see that road there?" he asked as he pointed toward my left.

I nodded, looking toward where he gestured.

"That's Kolekole Pass. We run that and do ruck marching, which is in full uniform with about fifty pounds of stuff in a rucksack. It's insane the first few times you do it." He shook his head.

"Can anyone run that or just soldiers?"

"No, anyone can. Why? Do you run?" Christian acted surprised.

"Yeah, I did around eight miles this morning, from my hotel up to Diamond Head. It was my only reprieve while I wasn't speaking with my mom. The one thing I did for myself." I felt my eyes fill with tears at the thought of my mother.

"Maybe we can run it together sometime."

We drove in comfortable silence until we arrived at Giovanni's Shrimp truck.

Parked in the middle of what looked like the front yard of somebody's home and, surrounded by several plumeria trees, sat the food truck. The shock of it being an actual automobile and the instantaneous doubt of the quality of food they served diminished at the number of people waiting in line. The ones that weren't in line were signing their names all over the truck.

*How exciting!*

What surprised me even more was that the crowds gathered there to eat weren't just tourists, there were tons of locals.

"Have you eaten here before?" I asked as we walked toward the truck.

"All the time. It's delicious, but I must warn you, it's not conducive for kissing." Christian laughed and gestured toward the picnic tables. It was a good look on him. "Go find us a seat and I'll get the food."

I found one of the only empty tables under the shade of a beautiful plumeria tree and watched as Christian made his way through the line to order our food. Stuffing our soda cans into the front pockets of his shorts, he carried our plates of food over to the table. The scent of garlic wafted through the air when he placed everything on the table. It smelled so good.

"Thank you," I said with a big smile.

"You're welcome."

My plate was filled with a mound of rice covered in shrimp, and all of it smothered in garlic sauce. Christian brought a few extra paper plates to house the shrimp shells as we removed them. It was a messy affair, but one that proved to be worth it. The food was delicious. I moaned in delight as the buttery garlic touched my tongue and I licked my fingers without shame.

"Oh my god, this is so good!" I exclaimed, humming in delight.

Christian shook his head with a slight chuckle, but seemed to enjoy it just as much as me.

"We are going to stink after this," I snickered with a finger in my mouth. "Hey, so, I've been wondering what the deal with Takata is. I mean, why do you guys ride him like that?"

His face turned serious again, like he'd put a mask on to hide his feelings and looked at me dead on.

"He's . . . a bit off. All the guys ride him because he walks around talking about his dragon. It's strange. I'm not sure how guys like him are even in the service. Imagine counting on him in battle and wondering if he knows the difference between reality and his dream world," he rambled while pointing to his temple.

I was in complete disbelief that the Army wouldn't know if someone was mentally unstable. Taking a deep breath in order to gather my words, I presented my question to him. "But if he was really that . . . out of it, they wouldn't let him stay in, right? I mean, he must be stable. Do you ever think he's just fucking with you?"

"No, because the kid's a fucking genius and I think he could get by enough. Look, don't get me wrong. He's a good kid and we like him well enough, but he's not someone I want to entrust my life to on the battle field." Christian shrugged.

After lunch, we drove down the street to a small North Shore beach and sat in the sand for a while. Christian was not a man of many words and I didn't have much to share about my life that I hadn't already told him. I wanted to know more about him: his family, his life before the military, but I just wasn't sure how to ask without seeming intrusive. So, instead I started with simple questions to get him talking and hoped he'd continue on his own.

"Where in New Mexico are you from?"

"Ruidoso. It's a small, tourist town near the Sierra Blanca Mountains. They're big on skiing in the winter and the town is a summer retreat for the Texans to escape from the heat."

"Hmmm. I've never been to New Mexico. Do you go back often?"

"At least once a year to visit my family. They come here more often, though."

"So, you've been based here the entire time you've been in the military?" I asked.

"Yes, ma'am," he said, smirking again.

It was getting late and Christian had to work the next day so we headed back to the base. While driving, I wondered if he'd done this a lot. I figured if he targeted tourists to date, he didn't have to see them again once they left. I supposed it was a great way to date for a man who might not want a commitment. I'd have to watch myself with him, to make sure I didn't let my feelings grow, and just take it for what it was.

# Chapter 9

## Focus

After a few days of not hearing from Christian, I decided not dwell on him and keep myself busy with sightseeing. I convinced myself it was better that way, though I just couldn't seem to release the thoughts running through my mind about not making the same mistakes as my mother. So in an effort not to follow in her footsteps, I had to stay away from him.

By not thinking about Christian, I was able to see more of the sights on my mother's list. One day was spent at the PCC — Polynesian Cultural Center. What an amazing place it turned out to be! It felt like I had visited every Polynesian island around. I learned their dances and the crafts they were known for creating. Also, I stayed late for the luau and was lucky enough to taste the amazing cuisine while being entertained with fantastic music and dancing.

A few days were spent just lounging around the pool, but every morning I ran to the volcano, pushing myself to run harder. Throughout the journey, my mind would wander back to Christian and each day that went by without seeing or talking to him created a growing ache in my heart. I couldn't help but miss him as the days passed. Something about his aloof behavior attracted me, even though I knew he was dangerous.

While I tried to keep my mind occupied by hiking through the lush trees in Waimea Valley, I found it difficult to not think about him. As I listened to the rush of the waterfalls dropping over the side of tall cliffs in torrents, I noted how it felt like such a romantic place. Standing at the top of Diamond Head volcano and looking out over Waikiki, I couldn't get Christian out of my mind. I felt ridiculous because he was just a random guy whom I didn't know very much about. In all honesty, he hadn't done anything to earn so much thought in the first place.

Another week went by without hearing from Christian. Time hadn't made it easier to forget about him, but I carried on and continued with my sightseeing.

One day, about two weeks since I had seen him, I found myself  at the swap meet being held in the Aloha stadium. I was just walking around and looking for things to buy. There were rows of vendors who offered everything I had seen at the International Market Place, but for cheaper prices. With my hands full of bags of chocolate-flavored coffee and some of those coconut-flavored macadamia nuts I had seen at the market place, I rounded a corner to go down the next isle and spotted Christian with his group of friends from the beach. Since it had been almost two weeks since I'd seen him,

I continued walking without acknowledging any of them. I almost made it to the end of the isle before I heard my name being called out by the familiar voice of Takata.

"Anela! Hey, how's it going?"

Turning around, I saw him standing alone, and I felt relieved. "Hi, Takata. I'm fine. How about you?"

"Good, good. Just shopping for some supplies. We come here at least once a month to pile up on goodies and clothes," he said.

"That's nice, but I have to go. I want to get a few more things before I head back to my hotel. It was nice seeing you," I grumbled and began walking away as fast as I could.

I didn't want to be rude, but I wanted to get out of there. Rounding the corner, I felt my heart beating through my shirt. I could see the heavy rise and fall of my tank top from the gasps of air I inhaled. Taking refuge inside one of the vendor's shops, I tried to calm myself down. When I peeked out, I saw a crowd of shoppers walking by but none of them were soldiers. With a hand on my chest to slow the beat, I began walking down the rest of the isle.

"Anela!"

Dammit, I knew that voice, which meant Christian was right behind me. Pretending I hadn't heard him, I kept walking. With a grab to my bicep, he swung me to face him.

"Hey, why are you ignoring me?" he asked.

"Please let go of me." I yanked my arm back and turned around to walk away.

"What the hell is wrong with you?" Christian yelled.

The question made me swing back around to face him. I could feel my face scrunch up in anger from his accusation. How dare he?

"Oh, I don't know. I guess it's too much to ask why I haven't heard from you in two weeks. Though, I should be happy because I'm sure those two dates we had were more than any other girl has ever had before. I bet they get a dinner and nice fuck out of it before they never hear from you again. At least I didn't get screwed over."

Turning back around, I headed for the edge of the stadium, and tried to find my way back to my car, but I had no idea where I parked. The stadium was a big circle surrounded by the parking lot. In all honesty, I shouldn't have been so upset about Christian not calling me. He never promised me anything or said we were dating, but for some reason, it did bother me. On some level, I thought I had made a friend and it had felt good.

Without any sense of direction, I wandered the parking lot for almost half an hour. To my surprise, when I found my car, I found Christian leaning against it. As if I wasn't pissed off enough, the thought that he found my car before me filled me with rage. Unlocking the door, I threw my bags in the back seat and moved to get in.

"You're not even going to talk to me about this?" he asked.

I ignored him.

"Come on, let me in so we can talk," Christian pleaded.

Sitting in the driver's seat, I contemplated whether I should give him another minute of my time or act like we'd never met. With a click of the locks, I let him in. The door opened and Christian slid in, the seat still adjusted to fit him.

"I'm sorry I haven't called you, but you know, the phone works both ways," he said, moving his left hand back and forth between us.

Then he ran his palms on the khaki, cargo shorts he wore. As I looked at him out of the corner of my eye, I could see the beads of moisture dripping down his hairline and the slight sweat mark on the front of his white polo shirt. I turned on the car so we could cool off with the air conditioner.

I just shrugged in reply.

"Look, I don't even know what I'm doing here," he muttered, causing my heart to sink. "I mean, this whole thing spells disaster. You're my Colonel's daughter, and you're leaving soon. I don't even date, anyway. So, I'm sorry that I wasted your time."

He made a move to open the door.

"You don't date?" I looked at him in awe. What did he mean by that?

Christian sighed and rested his elbows on his knees and leaned his face on his outstretched fingers. I could feel the annoyance rolling off him in waves. Moving around in my seat so I could face him better, my nerves began getting the best of me.

He lifted his head and looked at me. "No, I don't date. Don't get me wrong, I'm not celibate or anything. I just don't see the same girl more than once."

"Oh," I replied, feeling like the air had been sucked out of my world.

"Yeah. Look, I thought maybe I could try the whole dating thing, but I don't want to hurt you. You're a nice girl and seemed to have lost enough in your life. I don't want to add to your pain, too."

I scoffed because regardless of how soon it might have been, I was hurt.

"Well, thanks for telling me. So I guess this is it?" I waved a hand between us and hoped he'd leave so I could go sulk somewhere.

And, as much as I was expecting that he would, I was surprised when he opened his door and left without another word.

# Chapter 10

## Hope

Loss was a feeling I'd become very familiar with, one I had experienced a lot of in my short life. The loss of my mother, a father I never knew, and of my grandparents, who were the only extended family I'd ever had, had left a hole in my heart. I'd also lost friends and pseudo-aunts and uncles over the years, so this feeling wasn't new to me. Needless to say, it still hurt a great deal. The loss of my friendship with Christian felt strange. I shouldn't have been so upset about it, because we had only gone out twice and he was kind of a jackass, but I liked him.

Instead of worrying about him and trying not to drown myself in my losses, I kept myself busy while waiting for my father to come back. I found myself at the beach every day. While I loved lying out, I didn't want to get too much sun, so I always had some shade. Most of the beaches that were butted up against a hotel had an umbrella rental service and I always got one. I read several light books that weren't too intense and didn't take a whole lot of time to get through. To most, I bet I looked pathetic all by myself on the beach, but in all honesty, I enjoyed it.

When I received the phone call from Takata telling me that my father was back in town, I was pleased. Well, maybe it was more than that; I was nervous, happy, and excited, but more than anything, I was scared. My mind went through so many emotions, but the fear ate through me the most. *What if he didn't want me?*

Takata made some suggestions about how I could get in touch with my father without him breaking the rules and giving out his information. He couldn't give me Neil's number or address, but he could tell me where he might be later in the day.

The air conditioning in my room sent chills down my spine — or was it the anxiety I felt as I got ready to meet my father? I ran around after my shower, trying to figure out what to wear, not that it would make a difference in his acceptance of me. In the end, I picked out a pair of khaki shorts with a fitted white, lace T-shirt and topped it off with a few accessories: a pair of black and khaki ballet slippers, a black buckle cuff, a khaki one, and a colorful scarf around my neck. It was nice and light for the weather, but also dressy for the occasion. Gathering the packet of information my mother had left for me, I headed out to the base.

Forty-five minutes later, I once again found myself in the parking lot of the information center. Looking around first to make sure I didn't see Christian anywhere, I got out of the car. I laughed at myself because he'd spot this car a mile away and know it was me.

*Oh, well! He isn't my concern anymore.*

With slow, nervous steps, I made my to the office door and stepped inside. There was a man behind the counter with Takata, and I felt myself freeze in place. His face was familiar – I saw those features in my mirror every day. I could feel my chest heaving quickly again; the air had a hard time moving in and out, and I felt like I was suffocating.

"May I help you?" Takata asked, helping me get back to our plan.

I flashed him a look before I put my game face on.

"Oh, yes." I walked toward the counter and pulled out the envelope of information, placing it on the counter with trembling hands. "I'm looking for someone, a . . . um . . . a Colonel Neil McDonald."

I watched out of the corner of my eye as my father snapped his head up at the sound of his name.

Takata turned around and looked at Neil, pleading for help. Already a step ahead of him, he treaded toward me.

"What do you want with Colonel McDonald?" he asked.

"Oh, ah . . . well, you see, I think he's my father."

Nerves ran through me as I dropped the bomb. I could've smacked myself for it, but his reaction was priceless. He looked at me good and long, inspecting every inch of my face and when he got to my eyes, he froze.

"How old are you?" Neil pressed, still staring straight at me.

"Twenty-two, sir."

"Who's you mother?" he blurted out much too fast.

"Carla Alborn," I replied.

Neil squeezed his eyes shut and blew out a long breath, while he braced himself on the edge of the counter with both hands. I watched his knuckles turn white while his face went red. Was he angry? I flashed my eyes to Takata to gage his reaction and he seemed okay with this response from my father.

"I have a picture," I mentioned, picking it out of the pile of papers.

Neil's body gravitated toward me just a tiny bit and he opened his eyes. The picture seemed to be his main focus in that moment and I knew he wanted to see it better so I handed it over to him.

"Pack this stuff up and come with me," he told me, before turning back to the desk. "Takata, I'm leaving. If anyone looks for me, tell them I've gone home for the day."

"Yes, sir."

Once all of the papers were stuffed back in the envelope, Neil walked around the counter and dragged me outside by the arm. He pointed at my car and asked, "Is that what you're driving?"

I nodded.

Neil pointed to a black SUV and told me I was to follow him.

# Chapter 11

# Fulfillment

"Honey, is that you?" a woman called from somewhere inside the house we'd just entered. Just down the road from the information center was a small community of single homes. Some of the houses were ranch style, while others looked to be two story residences. They looked nice and well maintained. Most had been finished with wood siding but each one had a different color scheme. There were blue and grey houses, along with maroon and other hues. It looked just like any other neighborhood that one would find in any particular city in the states, but not what I expected to find in Hawaii.

"Yes. And I have someone with me," Neil answered.

He directed me toward the back of the house and into the kitchen. A tall woman stood in front of the refrigerator, pulling out a casserole dish. Her blonde hair had been pulled into a long braid down her back, and she was wearing what looked like boys' board shorts that hung down to her knees. They looked cute on her thin frame.

Neil cleared his throat before speaking again. "Babe, come sit down. I want to introduce you to someone."

The lady closed the refrigerator and turned around, her beauty striking me. Her young face had a nice tan to it and I could tell she wasn't wearing any make-up. With a pair of big brown eyes, she had a natural beauty.

"Oh, who's this?" she asked, an honest smile on her face.

Neil gestured to the chair for us to sit down and then shook his head, looking at me. "You know, I didn't even ask you your name."

I laughed before answering, "No problem. My name's Anela."

"Anela. That's a nice name. Did you know it means 'angel' in Hawaiian?" Neil wondered.

I shook my head no.

"Well, this is my wife Penny." My father gestured to her. She sat in silence waiting to find out who the heck I was. "So, tell us your story."

I looked at them both in shock. Neil had put me on the spot. It was now or never and I wanted to get to know him. So I did as he asked and told them my story, showing them all the paperwork and the picture. By the time I finished, Penny had tears streaming down her face and I worried she'd throw me out. However, she surprised me when she jumped up and ran to my side of the table, pulling me into a crushing bear-hug. Shocked and emotional, I returned the embrace, but I wasn't quite sure why she was hugging me.

Whispering into my hair, she murmured, "There, there; you're not alone anymore."

And in that moment — more than any during the past few months — I missed my mom. She could never be replaced, but it seemed that I had others to love me now. It was all so bittersweet.

Penny turned to Neil and gestured for him to join us, which he did. She passed me off to him and he hugged me with all of his might, caressing my hair as we rocked back and forth. Neil cleared his throat and pulled back, only for both of them to pull their chairs closer to me and we sat in a small circle.

"I'm sorry about your mom. I've thought a lot about her over the years." He scrubbed at his face with both hands.

Neil and Penny stared and watched my every move. It unsettled me, but I understood the desire. I wanted to stare at my father, too.

"She looks just like you, Neil. Gorgeous — and look at those eyes," Penny gushed.

"Those are her mom's eyes, but I have to say, she looks like my mother and, well, me." He sounded proud and I watched as his ears reddened.

Neil and Penny insisted I stay for dinner so we could get to know each other better. We asked questions back and forth between the three of us and I was happy at how accepting they were of me. I knew at some point, I'd want to talk to my father alone so we could speak of my mother.

As we ate, I asked, "Do you guys have any children?"

"No, we tried for a long time before we found out I couldn't have any," Penny answered and her shoulders sagged a bit. "We've been married for fifteen years and figured that, being older and after trying so long, thought that was the way it was supposed to be. We didn't want to push it and be in our fifties with multiples, so we didn't go with any fertility treatments."

I hummed a sympathetic apology. "I'm so sorry."

"You know, things happen for reasons we have no control over, and a long time ago, I gave up trying to fight it. I realized that if I just gave in to fate, it would take care of me," she explained, holding onto my hand.

Penny and Neil seemed like such kind people so far, and it warmed my heart that I would have a chance at having a family again, but it also saddened me that my mother wasn't here to share this moment with me. Just as I was about to agree with her about fate, their doorbell rang.

"I'll get it, and then maybe Anela and I can take a walk, yeah?" Neil suggested.

Penny jumped up and put her right hand to her chest. "Anela, you must excuse my manners. Let me get you some tea."

She bustled around the kitchen, pulling two glasses out of the cabinet and the tea from the fridge, pouring some, and setting the glasses on the table.

"Thank you, Penny. I hope I am not disrupting any plans you two might have had."

"Oh, no. We were just settling back in. We arrived home yesterday from visiting our families in Connecticut. It's a lot of traveling in one day," Penny assured me.

I nodded as thoughts of more family ran through my mind. She must have read my mind because once again she got excited.

"Wait until they all hear about you. They will be so pleased and excited. They'll insist you go there to meet them. You just wait and see. You'll have so much family, you'll go crazy." She laughed.

"Do you really think so? I mean, they won't think less of me because my mother didn't tell them that she was pregnant? I'm just so unsure about this whole thing; it's all made me so nervous. I've wanted this my whole life and —"

The sound of my father's voice shut me up and Penny and I stayed quiet, listening to what was going on in the foyer.

"First Sergeant," my father greeted his visitor.

"Sir." The familiar voice caused me to freeze, wondering what in the world Christian was doing here.

"Come in. What can I help you with today?"

"I saw Anela's car outside and was hoping I could see her for a moment," he told Neil.

The palpitations began in my chest again.

"You know my daughter?" Neil asked.

"Yes, sir. We went out of couple of times and I've been trying to call her all day but she hasn't answered my calls. Well, to be honest, sir. I heard she was here and came to check for myself, hoping to catch her before she left," Christian explained.

Crap, I did notice I had two missed calls from him. I was in no shape to answer his calls while worrying about meeting my father. At least not after the way we left things.

"Well, that's up to her, First Sergeant. Give me a moment."

Neil walked back into the kitchen and asked me if I wanted to speak with Christian. I looked from Penny to my father, hoping I'd find the answer, but I wanted to know what he wanted. I shrugged my shoulder up and walked to the foyer, finding Christian standing there in a nice pair of blue cargo shorts and a short sleeve button down shirt. The hints of blue from the lines on the shirt really made his crystal eyes stand out. I stood there, unmoving. Not only was I surprised he was there in my long-lost father's house, but I was happy about it, too.

"Hi," I said, waving like a spaz and making myself look like an idiot.

"When I mentioned you weren't answering my calls, Takata told me you were here. I want to talk to you," he muttered.

For once, I could see how nervous he was as his hand moved from rubbing his neck to scratching the nape of his hair. It snapped me out of my nervousness quickly and made me feel more confident.

"Okay, about what?" I probed.

"I'm sorry about the last time we saw each other. I need to explain to you why I freaked out." Christian was still fidgeting. "You see, I've never been in a relationship before nor had I wanted to be in one. And even though I'd just met you, I wanted to try. The feelings came on so fast and it freaked me out, not to mention the fact that you live on the mainland. So, yeah."

I barked out a disbelieving scoff.

"You think you have problems? I told you my life story. You know about my parents and what my mother did. I'm afraid of loss, and not even sure I know how to love. So, on top of all that, you think I haven't thought about what will happen when I go home? But I really liked you, and you let me down." I sighed, unsure if I wanted to continue this conversation with him. "Why are you telling me this now?"

"Because I've missed you. I'd like for us to try to get to know each other better and take it from there. That is, if you'll give me another chance."

I stared into his eyes, trying to gauge his sincerity. "I guess we need to be patient with each other, right? And I'll need to come to terms that my high hopes for finding a fairytale-type love have been squashed?" I asked, half joking, and half serious.

Christian chuckled. "Well, I don't know about all that, but yeah, patience is a virtue, you know?"

*Smart ass!*

"You know, I was beginning to enjoy our newfound friendship and I think if we started from there again, I'd be okay with it," I said.

"That sounds like something I can handle. So, you'll answer my calls now?"

I laughed. "Yes, I will."

"Good. Well, I'll let you get back to, you know . . ." He waved toward the kitchen.

"Thanks. Bye, Christian."

He graced me with his dazzling smile before he walked toward the kitchen to say goodbye to Neil and Penny.

# Chapter 12

## Enjoyment

After the delicious dinner Penny made us, Neil and I went for a walk around his little military neighborhood. He tucked my arm through his and made some small talk, telling me about his family. His parents were elderly but still had control of their senses and he couldn't wait to tell them about me. Neil wanted me to meet them soon.

The whole situation felt surreal and made my head spin, but I wanted it all. I wanted to absorb every single word my father spoke, to memorize every crease and wrinkle that moved with each expression he made. I'd need to have those memories when I was back in California, all alone in my little cottage. I pushed out a big, cleansing breath and tried not to think about that, not when I didn't have to yet. Besides, right now I had more important things to worry about, like getting to know my father.

"Neil, um, I wanted to know — would you be okay with it if I called you 'Dad'?"

We'd made it to the end of the block and he'd stopped short. I felt his body stiffen, which kicked in my flight instincts because I thought I was being rejected. However, he wouldn't let my arm go. Instead, he turned to me and looked at me straight on. It was then I saw the tears in his eyes. His hands gripped on my arms and he pulled me into an embrace.

"Nothing would make me happier. Thank you — thank you so much, Anela," he exclaimed with so much emotion that I could sense his sincerity.

My body relaxed and I leaned in, returning his hug. Neil was tall and a little soft around the middle but not too much. In truth, it felt like he was in good shape. He pulled back and leaned his head down to wipe his eyes on his shoulder, alternating from one side to the other.

"Okay, let's keep walking," he murmured.

With my arm tucked back in his, we crossed the street and walked back toward his house but on the opposite side from where we started.

"Will you tell me what you remember of my mother?" I asked.

"Hmm. I remember the first time I saw her. She was beautiful and instantly caught my attention. I was with a couple of buddies at the PCC." He looked down at me. "The PCC is the Polynesian Cultural Center."

I laughed. "I know. I've already been there. Loved it so much."

Neil appeared pleased and continued to speak. "She was with a couple of girls and I'll never forget how beautiful she looked. Her long, black hair shimmered in the sunlight. She was standing on the little bridge that crossed over a small pond, leaning against the rope, and talking with so much excitement. Her face was lit up with happiness and her hands were flapping around. My buddies and I started walking across the bridge so I could get a better look at her and I was stunned. Her eyes — the same eyes you have, Anela — were captivating. When I looked at her, I was drawn in like a magnet and couldn't have backed away if I tried." He paused for a few moments, caught in the memory. "Even though my buddies didn't think I would, I approached her. I was shocked when she accepted a date with me. And, as they say, it was all history from there. My biggest regret was not insisting she give me her contact information. She took mine, but never used them because I never heard from her again."

I shrugged. "She told me she loved you, you know. I mean, if it's any consolation."

"There will always be a part of me that will love her. That's why it took me so long to get married. Penny knows all about Carla. I had to tell her. Penny and I had been friends since junior high and I couldn't lie to her about where my heart had been for the longest time. Then one day, the pain just vanished and it didn't hurt so much to think of your mother. I was able to move on and see Penny as more than just a friend. We married a few months later and have been very happy ever since." Neil cleared his throat. "Why don't you tell me how you know First Sergeant Sivers?"

That sudden change in topic made me laugh out of nervousness.

"Well, talk about not beating around the bush." I nudged his shoulder and he shrugged. "We met at the beach, through Takata. I think I like him a lot. The first couple of days after we met we seemed to hit it off, but then things didn't go so well. He freaked out and I was bummed out. We stopped talking to each other."

"I hope you don't mind me trying out this dad thing, but I'd like to start with some fatherly advice. Sivers is — or I hope "*was*" or he'll be answering to me — a ladies' man. But I'm sort of impressed with him having the gall to come over here and ask to speak with you. So, just be careful or I'll have to break his legs." He chuckled, his deep baritone tone vibrated down through my arm.

Before we knew it, we were back at his house. Penny had made us some coffee and homemade macadamia and chocolate chip cookies. The three of us would probably look like a bunch of loons to the outside world with the way our huge smiles never left our faces.

"When do you go home?" my dad asked.

*My dad*, I said to myself. *Wow, I liked the sound of that.*

"I have a little less than a month left of my vacation," I told him.

"Good. There's a family picnic in a couple weeks since all our units are now home. I'd like you to come so I can introduce my daughter to everyone." While he spoke, his smile never left his face.

"Wow, thank you. I'd love to. Do I need to bring anything?" I queried.

"I'll be making a few dishes, so you don't need to worry about a thing," Penny replied.

"Well, can I come over and help you?" I offered, searching for any way to help.

"Of course. You can come over anytime. This is your home now, too," she said.

My eyes watered from the simple sentiment.

∽∾

Over the next two weeks, Christian and I spent a lot of time together. We talked and really tried to get to know each other better. His honesty when we revealed our deepest secrets and insecurities was refreshing. It felt good to hear his doubts, but more than anything it felt good to speak about my own terrors. Losing everyone you'd ever loved was scarring and it made me want to hang on tight to what I had. The fears of loss still existed — it was all I knew — but I wouldn't let that stand in the way of my happiness, even if my need to keep everyone close made me come off as needy and clingy. How ironic would it be to lose everyone because I held on too tight, afraid of losing them?

Neil and Penny spent a lot of time with me, too, and Christian would join us when he could. The best day during my trip happened when my dad, Christian, and I went running on Kolekole Pass. Of course, we weren't bogged down with rucksacks, but it was a difficult run nonetheless. I was amazed that Neil kept up with us and I enjoyed having different scenery to admire, instead of the same view I'd had on my usual run. It was a nice change from Diamond Head.

Christian took me snorkeling at Hanauma Bay. I had a blast swimming with turtles that were almost bigger than me and looking at all the differently colored fish. After we snorkeled in the bay and looked at all the beautiful coral, we sat on the sand to relax a while. I snuggled into Christian's arms, allowing him to hold me close. With my head resting on his chest, I looked up at and our eyes met. I watched as his gaze flickered between my mouth and eyes, and I wondered if he would finally kiss me. His head lowered toward mine but seemed hesitant while he hovered over mine. Then I felt it, the warmth of his lips when they touched mine. Soft and slow at first, his kiss was gentle. His hands skimmed up my arms to my face where he cradled my head. With my eyes closed, stars flashed behind my lids. Christian's mouth opened and the pressure intensified. I tasted the salt from the ocean and felt the roughness of leftover sand. The fresh sea air lofted around us and mixed with our passion. After a loving peck, he placed his forehead against mine and stared into my eyes. I knew then that I was falling in love with this man.

After that, we couldn't get enough of each other. Every time we were together, we felt the need to touch the other's body. We'd sneak kisses when we thought my dad wasn't looking, or spend the entire evening on the beach necking and trying to get to know one another. Christian left me breathless every time.

A few times, we'd gone on double dates with Neil and Penny. Holding hands, we strolled around Waikiki and ate a wonderful dinner at Duke's. This restaurant was named after Duke Kahanamoku, who was famous for winning five Olympic medals in swimming. He was born on Oahu and grew up on the beaches of Waikiki, where he learned to swim and surf. Later in his life, he did some acting in Hollywood and made surfing popular on the mainland. Finally, he became a sheriff in Honolulu. Duke was such an icon to the local Hawaiians because of all of his accomplishments and became known to the locals as one of the original beach boys — not to be confused with the music group. A statue of him had been erected on Waikiki beach in his honor.

On another night, my parents took me to the Aloha Towers for happy hour and to window shop, but my favorite time with them was at the Sea Life Park. It was a once in a lifetime experience to swim with dolphins. It had always been a dream of mine and now I had pictures to document the wonderful day, along with the embarrassment on my dad's face when he had to kiss one of the dolphins. It was perfection! Christian — the flirt that he was — had no problems kissing his female dolphin.

One Tuesday night, Christian took me dancing at the local club, Zanzabar, and surprised me with an unknown talent. It started with the distinct drumbeats and trumpets of my favorite music to dance to: salsa. However, the confused look on my face faded in an instant when he dragged me out and swung me around the dance floor. Not only did he know how to salsa dance, but also he danced like a professional. Everyone has a unique style to their movements so I watched him work his feet for a moment and then matched him step for step, allowing the music to guide my movements. My hips moved along with the beat and my feet shimmied like hummingbird wings. When we'd hold hands, Christian would pull me toward him and I'd feel every inch of his body pressed against mine. Then, he'd push me out and twirl me, only to pull me back against him again. I felt like I was under a spell, like the sensual movements we made and the look in his eyes were piquing all of my senses. Our feet never faltered, and it felt like we'd been dancing together forever. We danced almost every song, only taking breaks to go to the bathroom or to get drinks.

By the end of the night, I was hot and my skin felt like it had been lit by a live wire. The desire to devour Christian was overwhelming, something I had never felt before. I wanted to leave — I wanted more, but I didn't know what that meant.

"Christian," I whispered in his ear.

He pulled me close to him and we danced as one.

"Let's get out of here." I nibbled his ear and felt a shiver pass through him.

He pulled back, looking in my eyes for an answer that he must have found, because he grabbed my hand and almost dragged me out of there.

# Chapter 13

## Desire

Anticipation and nervousness ran through me as I fumbled with the key to my hotel room. Christian wrapped his arms around my waist and rested his chin on my shoulder. The door flew open from our combined weight and we scurried in, slamming it shut with our bodies. Our lips connected and we took from each other as if we were the last drink of water in a dessert.

Christian's hand cupped my face.

"Anela," he whispered into my mouth.

I hummed in question not wanting to release his lips.

A rush of bravery hit me once more and I reached for his hand, leading him to the bed. Pulling him down with me, our hands began to explore as we pulled off the other's clothes. Our shoes fell with a clunk when they landed on the floor. Christian pulled me up to the pillows and knelt between my legs. His fingers skimmed my neckline with feather-like touches. He pushed up my sequined tank top and bent down to trail his lips across my stomach, causing goose bumps to spread over my skin. Slowly, he inched my shirt up higher until he needed me to lift up so he could remove it.

With expertise, Christian reached behind me and snapped open my bra with two fingers and pulled it off. I could feel the heat flush over my body as he gazed at me. I lay there, watching and waiting to see what he would do next. I tried not to rush him, but I needed more. My body called to his with every heave of my chest and breath that kept me alive. And then a thought struck me and the words tumbled from my mouth.

"You know — you know I've never done this before, right?"

A slight smile graced his face and he answered, "I know, angel. I've got you. You trust me, don't you?"

"Of course I do."

The moonlight poured in through the balcony doors and lit his eyes. Christian's gaze was so intense and my skin alive that when he reached for my skirt, my entire body shuddered. His crooked, closed-mouth smile grew on his face; he knew me well enough to know how his touches affected me. I was on fire, waiting for more. All the while, he teased me with light strokes near the places my body called for him, but never giving in to my needs.

"Please," I begged.

Christian scrambled off the bed and I was about to scream at him, but I didn't need to. With great speed, he took off his clothes and threw them on the closest chair, but not before he pulled some foil packets from his pants pocket and laid them on the nightstand. Christian climbed up next to me, showcasing his glorious body. I had never seen a man fully naked before and had nothing to compare it to, but he looked perfect to me. He had a narrow waist, lean hips, and long, muscular legs. The hard, warm muscles of his smooth, hairless chest, made me want to run my tongue over every centimeter of him. His musky scent was stronger from sweating and it spurred me on. I reached up and kissed his mouth with a hungry urgency, pulling him on me as I lay back on the pillows.

There wasn't an inch of my body that he didn't sample.

"Mmm, you taste so good," he murmured.

He played my body over and again, and in return, I kissed, licked, and touched every inch of him that I could reach. It couldn't have been soon enough before my wanting became a reality.

"Angel, this is going to hurt but it'll go away and I'll make you feel good. I promise," he murmured, with his forehead pressed against mine.

"I know. It'll be okay. But I just want you to know . . . that I love you," I whispered, because there was no other reason I'd give myself to him.

He reclaimed my mouth with a long, drugging kiss. As our bodies connected, I tried not to focus on any pain that might occur. Instead, I lost myself by watching his face contort from the pleasure my body gave him. From that, I endured it all until the discomfort subsided.

"Oh, God, Anela," he moaned, through clenched teeth.

My hands grasped his shoulders, holding him close to me until I was okay. "I'm good. Move."

And without a second to ponder he began slow, languorous thrusts, but it wasn't enough.

"More," I pleaded with him.

Christian delved deeper with each rhythmic push and I arched in unspeakable ecstasy. He let out small grunts with each lunge and I moaned through the pleasure. With every shift of his hips, he pushed me closer to the edge. He captured my mouth in another intoxicating kiss until I cried out from the lightning bolts of pleasure that jolted through me. I felt his movements become more sporadic and I knew he was getting close.

"Anela," he called out. "Oh, God, I love you. I love you."

The words shot from him like out of control fireworks, pushing him to his release.

"That was incredible." He let his body cover mine while we both lay there limp and sated.

"Is it always like that?" I asked, running my fingers up and down his back in lazy circuits.

Christian rolled off me, but pulled me close. "No, I don't think so. It's never been so incredible for me, angel. It's us — together — our connection that made it so special."

I slapped his shoulder, teasing him. "You already have me. There's no need to try and woo me anymore, you know?"

His jaw tightened and his eyes burned with fire. "That's not what I'm doing and you know it. I wouldn't say shit like that if I didn't mean it," he grumbled.

"Easy. I was just kidding."

He pecked my lips. "I do love you. That I know for sure." Christian's hand caressed my face with such adoration, it brought tears to my eyes. "I'll be right back."

He got up and went into the bathroom, returning with a warm facecloth and began to wash me with such care. Climbing back up, he pulled the covers down and laid them over us. He wrapped himself around me and held me tight. It was the most comforting feeling in the world.

"We need to sleep. We have the picnic tomorrow. Good night, my angel."

The next morning, I dropped Christian off at the barracks, leaving him with a searing kiss and a promise to meet at my dad's house later. The picnic didn't start for a few hours, but I had told Penny I'd help her prepare the food she decided to bring.

Before I was out of my car, the front door swung open and my dad stood, almost like he'd been anticipating my arrival. Neil jogged down the steps, capturing me in a hug. It had only been two days since I'd seen him, but it felt good to be wanted by him.

"Hey, kiddo. I missed you," he said, guiding me into the house. "God, I don't know what I'm going to do next week when you go back to California. I just got you."

My throat felt like someone had tightened a vice grip around it, and tears pricked my eyes. I didn't want to go home, but what I really wanted was to be asked to stay. I wouldn't feel right asking if they'd want me here permanently. There was nothing for me to go back to California for except an empty house. Without a family or a job, it didn't fit in the "attractive options" category.

I could only manage to croak out, "I know."

The last thing I wanted to do right then was cry about what I'd be losing. I wanted to have a good day with them and add to the wonderful memories I had made over the summer.

"Come on. Let's go see Penny," he replied, leading me into the house.

"Neil, is that Anela with you?" Penny yelled from the kitchen.

"It's me, Penny," I answered with a few lingering cracks in my voice.

When I walked in, I found her bent over the counter, cutting vegetables. Every bit of space in the kitchen had something on it.

"Hey, hon. I'm glad you're here. Can you peel those potatoes for me?" She pointed with the tip of the knife toward the table where two bags sat.

I walked toward her and gave her a side squeeze. "Of course. I'm on it."

The three of us worked in harmony as if we'd done this a million times. The warm feeling of family time moved me; it was so surreal and amazing.

Four hours later, Christian arrived and swept me up in a kiss that curled my toes. We piled into my dad's pick-up truck and drove to Kalakaua Community Park. My nerves were starting to set in and I clung to Christian's side, which seemed to be fine because he wouldn't let go of my hand. After we helped Penny place the food on the buffet table, Christian lugged me to a group of people off to the side. The men and women gathered there were chatting it up, and I spotted Takata's familiar face.

"Come, I want to introduce you," Christian whispered in my ear.

"Okay," I echoed back.

"What's up, everyone?" he bellowed when we walked up to them.

About half the guys standing in the crowd answered him at the same time. Christian was smooth as he fist bumped and half man-hugged some of them.

"Hey, Sivers. What's up, man?"

"Yo, dude, how's it hanging?"

"S'up?"

"I want you all to meet my girlfriend, Anela," Christian bragged and, all of a sudden, the women became interested in the conversation.

I was introduced to about fifteen wives; each of them told me their names and who they were married to. So far they all seemed nice, but we were women. The cattiness would come out sooner or later.

The afternoon was busy and filled with fun. Neil and I participated in the sack race, coming in second place. We all played tug of war, ran in the relay races, and a ton of other picnic-type games. The men were very competitive and they seemed to go crazy in order to get the win.

Penny helped ease my way in with the other wives and we laughed at the guys who pouted when they lost. I actually felt like I could fit in there, even more so when the majority of the wives commented on how Christian had never looked so happy, and how he never brought a girl around.

When he was too far to touch me, I'd catch him watching my every move. I found it endearing and sweet. No one had ever cared about me that much and I was extra lucky, because my dad was acting similarly, though in a fatherly way. The guys from Neil's unit introduced themselves and congratulated me on finding my father and making him happy. It was a win-win for all of us.

# Chapter 14

## Trustworthy

I was full of love — packed to the brim with emotion. Sentiments I had never felt before were running through my every essence, making me feel scared, happy — and insane. I spent as much time as I could with Christian, Neil, and Penny during my last week in Hawaii. Every night, Christian would stay with me and then leave early the next morning to report for work at the base. He claimed he didn't mind, because he wanted to make the most of our time together.

*Ugh!* When he said things like that, my heart hurt. It was hard hearing how much he would miss me or how he wished I didn't have to leave, but he never took it one step further. My dad and Penny were the same way. They'd make sly comments about how they would miss me or they wished I wasn't leaving. Time was ticking down and I needed one of them to tell me that they wanted me to stay.

The emotions soaring throughout my body managed to double — no; *triple* — because my last day in Hawaii had arrived. I was scheduled for the five o'clock flight out and had to check in two hours prior to departure. The urge to burst into tears at any given moment overwhelmed me. I hadn't made many future plans, either. Neil and Penny had asked me to go to Connecticut with them so I could meet my grandparents. They also invited me to come back and visit as soon as I could. Christian, like my father, didn't get much time off so he wanted to know how soon I could return, but otherwise, everything had been left in the air and I felt like my life was in limbo. Why was I too proud to ask to stay? Couldn't I just ask them if they wanted me here?

I didn't know; maybe I was afraid of the rejection if they said no. That would be the last straw for me, most likely killing what was left of my soul. Finding my father had been an amazing experience and it had brought me so much joy. It didn't mean I had forgotten what I'd lost when my mother died — the pain was still so fresh and the guilt all-consuming — but I decided to live my life to the fullest.

So while I sat at my dad's kitchen table crying, laughing, and memorizing every special moment with my family, I dreaded the thought of leaving. Neil and Penny were treasures, and they had responded to my sudden intrusion into their lives by welcoming me with open arms. The way Neil took his newfound responsibility as the father of a twenty-two year old woman was admirable. Penny was so selfless and had been willing to accept her husband's illegitimate child. However, looking at the big picture, they'd accepted me so easily — and I was lucky — but I had to leave it all behind. I had to go back to my mother's house and to a job I didn't have. I would have to go back to nothing.

Rain began pelting against the roof. The rain in Hawaii was so different from the drizzling gloom that I was used to in California. The sky would open up and the droplets would fall for about fifteen minutes, all while the sun would shine  and a beautiful rainbow would arch through the clouds. Droplets fell two by two from the big lush leaves mimicking the tears that welled up in my eyes at the thought of leaving everything behind. I watched as the stunning flowers drooped low from the weight of the moisture as if they were hanging their heads in mourning. The glass doors that led to the veranda framed the multicolored rainbow shooting across the sky. It was such a lovely place to find myself, and thanks to my mother, I had been afforded that opportunity.

The doorbell rang, breaking me from my reverie. I jumped a mile high, almost running over my dad to get to the door. I was eager to see Christian. Everyone wanted to see me off at the airport, so they decided Christian would ride with me while Neil and Penny followed us. I'd drop off my car at the rental agency and we'd go to the airport with my dad. I swung the door open and jumped into Christian's arms, wrapping my legs around his waist and locking him in my embrace.

"Oomph! I take it you missed me?" he asked with a chuckle.

"Yeah," I whispered into his neck.

I felt something poking my cheek as it rested against his shoulder and pulled back to see what it was. My mouth dropped open and I felt my eyes bulge out. Before I could think, I jumped down and stood back, just taking in the sight before me. I wouldn't be surprised if I was drooling. My man — my handsome man — was dressed in his Class A's and looking mighty fine, I might add. The uniform had a navy blue jacket with royal blue pants. He was delicious from the beret on his head to the shine on his shoes. My heart thumped through my breastbone and I struggled to breathe. I looked up, turning bright red because he was watching me with such amusement.

"You like?" he wondered with his crooked, cocky smile.

I shook my head. "No, I love," I said with a smile and reached out to run my fingers over the stripes on his sleeve. He had five stripes: three on the top and two on the bottom. "What's the occasion?"

"Just wanted to send you off in style, angel."

I pulled him into the house so he could say hello to my parents. We had a nice lunch but then it was time to leave. My car was already packed with my luggage and I'd checked out of the hotel when I left in the morning. I looked prepared, but there was no way I was ready to leave.

# Chapter 15

## Love

"Goodbye, Dad. I'm going to miss you so much," I cried into Neil's chest.

He rubbed my back and tried to console me but I was hysterical. I knew this was going to happen, that I'd lose control and sob like a baby.

"I'm going to miss you, too, but we'll see each other soon. Believe me, I just got you. I'm never letting you go again," he murmured.

But the truth was that he *was* letting me go and I wasn't handling it well.

My sobbing-induced hiccups caused Penny to rush over and join our hug. She caressed my hair and whispered sweet words into my ear. Always such a nurturer, her gentleness only made me cry harder.

"Come on, honey. You don't want to miss your flight. We'll see you soon. I promise," she whispered, soothingly.

I wanted to tell her that I didn't care if I missed my flight, but decided to just go with it.

Hugging Neil and Penny one last time and promising to see them in Connecticut soon, I turned and faced Christian. He stood off to the side, watching us say goodbye and letting us have one last moment together. When he walked toward me, I fell into his arms. He gave me one hard squeeze before he pulled away, only to cup my face with his hands. His mouth met mine in a fury of heat and passion. The kiss spoke of how much he loved me, how much he'd miss me. Moving my lips against his, I returned the sentiment. I stepped back, and with one last wave to everyone, I walked into the airport.

Once it was time to board my flight, I squeezed through the people putting their bags away and looking for their seats. It was chaos, but I just kept going until I arrived at my seat, which was in the last row. I put my bag up into the storage bin, sat down, buckled my seatbelt, and decided I'd go to sleep right away, figuring that if I was asleep, I couldn't think about everything I was leaving behind. It would help me forget my broken heart for at least a little while.

I wasn't sure how long I'd slept, but I awoke to the sound of the engines pushing us through the air and a quick peek out the window showed white puffy clouds. Then I realized it had been an announcement that woke me up.

"Ladies and gentlemen, we would like to thank you once again for flying with us. We have a special treat for you today," one of the flight attendants announced.

I leaned my head back and closed my eyes, just waiting to hear what kind of treat we were receiving. I hoped it was free liquor or a bottle of wine because at that moment, I'd love nothing more than to get drunk.

Before I could figure out where it was coming from I heard someone singing. I couldn't tell if it was someone singing live or a song playing over the airplane radio, so I leaned my head out into the aisle and looked back into the little space where the flight attendants sat. No one was there so I looked up the long aisle toward first class, but I couldn't see anyone there, either.

*Oh, well*, I thought.

Leaning back again, I tried to relax to the music. The male voice was singing about how much he loved kissing his girl when she slept, how happy he was that they'd met, and how he wanted her to be his forever. A moment later, the feel of the song changed. Instead of all the things he was happy about, he began to sing about all the things he'd do for his girl.

"I love you with all my heart and I've loved you from the start. I'll love you forever and I can promise I'll leave you never," the voice sang, smooth as silk.

The song was so beautiful that it brought tears to my eyes. I planned to ask the flight attendant what the name of the song was the next time I saw her.

"I've allowed my feelings to be unfurled and now I want to give you the world. You're my love, my life. Will you please be my wife?"

My eyes flew open because those last words had not been sung; they were spoken by a voice I was very familiar with. I stuck my head out into the aisle again, searching for someone to tell me what the heck was going on. There — still in his Class A's — stood Christian with a hopeful smile on his face. He walked toward me at the same time he beckoned me to come to him with his arms. He didn't have to ask me twice. I popped my seatbelt open and jumped out of my seat, meeting him half way.

"Hi," he whispered. Though Christian's face was burning red, his perfectly crooked smile was still dazzling on his face.

"Hi." I giggled, because I had no idea how he'd gotten on this plane without me knowing. My throat closed as I began to choke up. My heart was filled with so much love and happiness.

Christian knelt down on one knee, doing the best he could in such a small space. He was almost on top of the people sitting in the seats next to him.

"Anela, I love you with all my heart," he began, struggling to open the ring box he had pulled out of his jacket pocket. "And I'll always love you. There's nothing I want more than to spend the rest of my life with you. As your time to leave got closer, I felt my world crashing down around me. It's not something I wanted to deal with and I knew I had to change that. So here I am, on one knee, hoping that you'll marry me."

I wanted to laugh at him because he was too cute. My man of little words had just said so much and each one of them was worth a million.

Looking him in the eyes and with all the love I had inside of me, I answered him with a resounding, "Yes, yes! Of course I'll marry you."

Tears streamed down my face when — with trembling hands — Christian slipped the white gold, pear-shaped diamond ring on my finger, stood up, and kissed me as everyone on the plane cheered, hollered, and hooted for us.

# Epilogue

## Everything

"I do apologize for the inconvenience, sir, and we will correct the issue promptly. In the meantime, allow us to comp your dinner tonight," I said to the unhappy customer in front of me.

"Thank you, we appreciate it. And I hate to complain, but my wife was not happy. After being gone all day, she expected the room to have been cleaned and to have fresh towels." He shrugged.

"I apologize again. Have a good evening and thanks again for choosing to stay in The Hilton Hawaiian Village. We'll do what we can to make your stay pleasurable," I replied.

I typed a few things into the computer before walking back to my office. My workday had flown by and now it was time to go home. I closed my office up for the day and ran to my car like the quick movement would get me home faster. As excited as I was to go to work every day, the anxiousness to return home each night raced through me with the same fervor.

Parking my car in the driveway, I couldn't help but think how surreal my life was right now. I'd had five years to get used to it, but when loss was such a commonality in your life, it became ingrained. I now possessed everything I had ever wanted and feared I'd lose it all every day.

"Momma!"

I heard the screeches coming from the front door. There stood Penny with my handsome little boy in her arms. Calvin Neil Sivers looked exactly like me, eyes and all. The champagne fuzz he had when he was born grew out to a thick head of blond hair. The grayish blue eyes all babies had when they were born turned into my yellow cat eyes — although, he did have his daddy's side smirk. God, he was going to be a heart breaker. Jumping out of the car, I practically broke through the door in excitement to get to him. I extended my arms out to him and he reached back for me.

"Hey, baby. I missed you today. Were you good for Grandma?"

He nodded his little head and wrapped his arms around my neck. I held him close to me and ran my hand up and down his back. I looked up at Penny, who still stood in the doorway.

"Christian's not home yet?" I asked.

"He went down the street to help your dad fix some shelves in the pantry. They broke from too much weight," she said while shaking her head.

We made our way into the house. Penny loved to cook and their cabinets and pantry were always full of food. I'd bet she had cooked us dinner already. Most nights, she'd make enough for her, my dad, and us.

She had been my savior since I had moved to Hawaii. I owed her so much; I'd never be able to pay her back. Christian — of course — had followed me to San Francisco and helped me settle all of my affairs. Lennie assisted me with renting my house and promised to look after it for me. We were there for a week and flew right back to the base to arrange our wedding. I had to stay with my dad and Penny until we were officially married so we could qualify for family housing.

Penny helped us organize a small wedding. When Christian's family flew in for the big day, he promised me I had nothing to worry about after seeing the panic written all over my face. I thought they'd hate me since the first time they were meeting me was because of our wedding. However, he was right. They were all so sweet and supportive, however, and we'd been close ever since.

After we were married, I tried to be the typical Army housewife like Penny and the other wives were, but it just didn't work for me. In less than a month, I was going stir crazy and needed to find something to occupy my time. Ever the supportive husband, Christian pushed me to find something that would make me happy. I just didn't know what that was at the time so I went with something a bit more logical. I wanted to use my business degree and decided to get a Master's degree in Hospitality

Management. It couldn't have been more perfect for me. A year later, I had finished my classes, had a certificate, and went searching for a job.

With the horrible economy, travel was not a priority for many people, and although the island always seemed to be swarming with tourists, hotels were a dime a dozen. I knew getting a manager position right away wouldn't happen, so I applied for a job as a front desk clerk at The Hilton Hawaiian Village. I learned so much in that position and worked very hard at my job, proving that I could do more. It took me a little over a year to become a manager.

"Anela."

I heard my named cutting through my thoughts and opened my resting eyes to see my hunk of a husband standing before me with his classic smirk plastered on his face.

"Were you sleeping?" he asked.

"No, just resting here with Cal, thinking."

"Oh, yeah. What were you thinking about?" he prodded and sat down next to us. He placed his hand over mine and rubbed the baby's back with me.

Christian was an amazing father and spent every possible minute he could with our son. He was so happy and proud that Cal had my eyes and looked like me.

"How much my life has changed and how I'm the happiest woman in the world," I said, giving him a dazzling smile of my own — something I'd learned to do since we'd been together. Smiles like mine came naturally when you had a lot to be happy about.

Christian leaned in and kissed me on the lips. Calvin must have fallen asleep because he didn't stir. I looked down and leaned back to see his long blond eyelashes resting against his chubby little cheeks.

"Penny's ready for us to eat. Your dad will be here in a minute. You want to go put him down and get changed?" Christian suggested. I nodded and scooted forward to get off the sofa.

Being careful, I climbed the stairs and went straight to Cal's room to lay him down. He stirred a little, but didn't wake up. Just watching him sleep brought butterflies to my stomach. The first few months of my pregnancy with him had been quite stressful. I had just been promoted to front desk manager and then, less than a week later, I found out I was three months pregnant. The fear and stress of telling my boss about my condition made me so sick that I almost lost the baby. I couldn't shake the feeling they'd fire me. Christian finally threatened me one day to either tell them myself, he'd do it, or he'd make me quit. When he reminded me of how it was affecting our baby, I broke down, put on my big girl panties, and spoke with my manager.

Thank goodness, she was genuinely happy for me. My concern about letting them down when they had just given me a promotion had been for nothing. They appreciated my hard work and knew I'd be back after the baby was born. I worked until the last possible minute and went back after taking six weeks of maternity leave. That wouldn't have happened if it weren't for Penny offering to babysit for us.

I skimmed my fingers down the side of the angelic baby face of my two year old before I went to my room to wash up. With a look around our bedroom, I laughed a little because my clothes were all over the place. Oh, boy — that was another story.

We had a beautiful, black, king-sized bed and a teal green sitting chair in the corner. The walls were painted a light yellow almost the shade of a bagel. The bonus of our room was the walk-in closet because we had plenty of hanging space and drawers. Our room wasn't very fancy and we didn't do a lot to decorate it. Our time was better spent with our baby and doing things as a family, instead of trying to keep up with the neighbors. Too many women spent their time showcasing their houses instead of appreciating the warm bodies that inhabited those homes with them.

However, I recalled how Christian and I hadn't adjusted very well in the beginning of our marriage. I couldn't stress about decorating when I had to worry about organizing and cleaning up after myself. My sloppy habits hadn't mixed well with his neat-freak tendencies. I swore he suffered from obsessive-compulsive disorder because all of his stuff had to be in their proper place and there was a certain way to display it. He expected me to follow suit but I didn't have time to make sure all the labels faced front or if things were in order by size. I decided to pick up my dirty clothes and place them into the dry cleaning bin so he wouldn't freak out. Christian had taught me to organize things better and I showed him how to relax.

Once we got used to each other, things calmed down. We fell into a routine, but the best of times was when we'd go to the beach with Cal. I made friends with a few of the wives and they'd join us with their families. We'd pack picnics and spend the whole day playing in the sand and splashing around in the water.

I heard the front door open and close and knew my dad had arrived. I changed from my work clothes, washed up, and ran downstairs so we could eat as a family, like we had almost every night.

I couldn't imagine myself any happier than I was right now. I met the man of my dreams, moved to a place that most considered paradise, and had a huge family.

My only wish was that my mother could have been around to see me get married, and meet her grandchildren and my wonderful husband, but I had a feeling she was watching us from heaven. None of this would have been possible without my mother and her request that I follow her footsteps.

## The End

# *Just Like in the Movies*

# By M.B. Feeney

# Acknowledgement:

Gaz, Hana and Joshua for letting me "work" even when it looked like I wasn't. Honestly, Facebook IS research. I love you all. The rest of my family, thanks for just accepting that this is what I do, no questions and seemingly no surprise either.

Sarah and Lea, thanks for pre reading and donning pom poms when I needed the support and motivation to get this finished. I got there in the end.

Elizabeth Lawrence and Sydney Kalnay... well, you survived my mess of Britishisms and general grammatical mess. I don't think I can ever thank the two of you enough for simply persevering. Also, the comments on the manuscript that made me laugh out loud made it all worthwhile to trawl through the sea of red.

# Chapter 1

## Act One, Scene One

"Come on, Ava," my best friend, Erica, called out, trying to hurry me along while I made sure my dogs had enough food and water for the evening. "We'll lose our reservation."

I didn't know why she bothered doing this every time we went out; we were *always* late. "You do realise that it's a pub, don't you, Davidson? They don't tend to honour reservations. Anyway, we've been going there every Wednesday for almost five years. Not only will they keep a table for us, they'll *expect* us to be late."

"Well, maybe we can surprise them by turning up when we said we would," she said with a huff, her blue eyes flashing with unconcealed frustration at my slow pace.

Once I'd locked the door behind me, I linked arms with her, and we began to walk the short distance to The Goose for our regular girls' night while my live-in boyfriend, Marcus, was at football training.

I'd met Marcus Tripp not long after joining Wilson Insurance. Although I'd never really fancied him, he was persistent. Our friendship had grown, and we'd fallen into a routine that suited both of us. I was happy with the attention, and the sex . . . yeah, it was okay. As time passed, the earth rarely moved when we were intimate; more often than not, it was pretty much over before it began. Still, we stayed together, more out of habit and familiarity than anything else. We did love each other. I just wasn't sure that it was enough.

In the evenings I spent alone, I would daydream about living the life of a lead in a Hollywood chick flick, but then reality would slap some sense into me. My life was as good as it was going to get. I wasn't about to be swept off my feet any time soon. Marcus and I were comfortable, and that was enough — for me, at least. I was too scared to ask Marcus what he felt.

We tried for a couple of years to have children, but it never happened. After many serious discussions, we decided to give up on the idea altogether. That was when we bought our first fur baby: a beautiful Collie cross called Rhea. She was our little girl, and we both doted on her. We assuaged our guilt over our mutual neglect by caring for Rhea, devoting our attention to another living being rather than to each other. The puppies, Remus and Romulus, soon joined her, and our "family" was complete.

For as long as I'd known him, Marcus had played Sunday League football, which was followed by an afternoon with his teammates at the very pub I was now approaching. Coupled with training one evening a week, his evenings out gave me more than enough time to spend with Erica or at home with the dogs.

"Have you thought any more about that holiday I mentioned?" Erica asked while we claimed our usual table. Our customary bottle of red wine was already ready and waiting for us.

"I have . . ." My words drifted away when I thought back to her idea of a girlie getaway on the Isle of Wight. Just as its name suggested, the top-class Lakeside Hotel with attached spa was located right next to a beautiful lake. Bliss.

"And? Why the hesitation?" Erica pushed like she always did, her blue eyes flashing once more as she looked into my brown ones.

The idea of a real getaway made the blonde hairs on the back of my neck stand on end, but I tried to rein in my excitement. "I don't know. It sounds amazing, and Lord knows I could do with some time away."

"Do it, then."

I knew I had enough holiday time available at work. *Screw it.*

"Let's do it."

While Erica parked her car, I gazed around at the stunning scenery in which the hotel was nestled. We would be calling this place home for the next three days, followed by ten days at a beachfront house in Ryde.

"How the hell have you managed to afford this?" I asked, looking around me in awe.

Erica had refused to let me pay anything towards the hotel, insisting that the holiday was her treat. I had been blown away by her generosity, but I demanded to help with the cost of the beach house, refusing to take 'no' for an answer.

"I told you; I had a bit of extra cash left over from when I was made redundant."

We hauled our suitcases out of the boot and began to walk towards the grand entrance. I stopped dead when I realised what she'd said. Her last job as a receptionist–slash–personal assistant to a financial advisor had ended amicably when the company had made the hard choice to let her and others go.

"Erica, that was three bloody years ago. You are not *that* good at saving, even with a half-decent payout." I looked at her, and then I remembered what other money she had and felt a little guilty.

"I squirreled some away. Stop giving me grief so we can get this weekend underway."

I couldn't help but at laugh at the stern look she attempted to give me. We entered the cool lobby, and immediately I felt my entire body begin to relax.

One mudpack and a full body massage later, Erica and I were on the terrace in the early evening sunshine, having a light dinner and glass of wine.

"I could get used to this," Erica commented while we watched the soft, warm breeze send ripples across the surface of the lake. It whipped Erica's dark hair around her face gently, the sunlight emphasising the red highlights. I'd never seen her so relaxed. My best friend was a 'grab life by the horns' kind of woman; she always had been. I'd often wished I could be like that, but I had the bad habit of over-thinking everything. I tended to try and please others rather than do things just for myself. That was probably the main reason I was still in a relationship with Marcus.

"It's beautiful out here, but a bit too quiet. I don't think I'd be able to get used to it." Marcus and I lived in a house that was situated just off a busy main road. It was the most direct route into the city centre, and a hospital lay in the other direction. Over the years, we had grown accustomed to the constant noise of traffic and ambulance sirens. The almost complete silence of my current surroundings unnerved me a little. "Still, the view is stunning."

"It's not for long; we'll hit the beach soon. I doubt it'll stay quiet this time of year."

I smiled at the thought of beachside living, for however short a time. It had always been a dream of mine to live by the sea, where I could cruise along at my own pace with my fur babies. I was still holding out hope for a lottery win to make it a reality.

"Have you got our itinerary all set up for when we reach Ryde?" I asked.

"Nope."

I looked at her in shock. Erica was a 'list' person: always referring to them, checking things off, and adding more important tasks or things to do. Not having our ten-day holiday organised down to the smallest detail seemed so out of character for her.

"Both of us need some serious downtime," she explained. "The one thing I will insist upon is at least one trip into town. Not only will we need to get some food, but there are a few pubs and clubs we can check out. Plus, there's this great bookshop I think you'll love."

"I reckon I can cope with that. How far from town will we be staying?"

"Five minutes by car; twenty if you fancy walking it."

Already, I was imagining myself going for my morning jog along the country roads. It was just a shame the dogs wouldn't be there to keep me company, but I'd packed my iPod.

"Less about that for now; we need an early night. Facials have been booked for first thing in the morning." Eric grabbed my hand to pull me out of my chair, and we headed inside and up to our room.

# Chapter 2

## Act One, Scene Two

I lounged in the passenger seat of the car while Erica drove from the hotel back towards Ryde. Through the open window, I watched the lush, green scenery pass us by. The air was so fresh; with every inhalation, I could almost hear my lungs performing an aria in high praise. My bare feet were resting on the dashboard so my legs could get a bit of colour from the bright sunlight.

Erica frowned a little at my feet, which were defiling the otherwise pristine surface, but she managed not to comment on them, instead asking, "Looking forward to doing as little as possible for the next ten days?"

"Like you wouldn't believe. Sun, sea, sand, and utter relaxation. Just what I need." I lifted my large sunglasses to wink at her and grinned.

She reached up with one hand to pull back her dark brown hair, which shone in the sunlight while the wind whipped it around her head.

"You and me both, sweet cheeks. I can't remember the last time I had a holiday . . . Oh yeah. It was my 'honeymoon'."

We both laughed at the memory of Erica's ill-fated marriage five years previous. She and Michael had been together for almost eight years and made a beautiful, disgustingly happy couple. They'd gotten married, and then swanned off to the Caribbean for a luxury honeymoon. The day before they were due to return home, she found him in bed with one of the pool boys. Needless to say, she came home alone and filed for an annulment before her tan had faded. It took her a long time to get over it, but the experience had made her stronger, if more distrustful of men.

"Well, I can promise not to hop into bed with anyone. I just want space and time to think and chill." I sighed and gazed back out the window.

"There'll be plenty of time for that."

"Remind me to get you a big thank-you present for organising this."

Rather than argue the way she normally would, Erica simply smiled before returning her full attention to the road ahead.

Just as we reached the outskirts of town, Erica made an executive decision and stopped to do some shopping, which saved us having to drive back for it later. We parked up outside the first supermarket we saw and went inside.

Shopping for food with Erica was much different than going with Marcus. With him, we bought only what we needed and left. When I was with Erica, we ambled around, checking out everything on offer. The way she saw it, we were on holiday and could eat what we wanted, guilt free. I was rather inclined to agree.

We filled up a trolley, paid, and then transferred our bags to the car before taking a quick walk around town. I spotted the bookshop that she had mentioned earlier at the spa.

"I'm just going in to have a quick look; I didn't bring any books with me," I told her. After we'd arranged to meet back at the car in thirty minutes, she headed towards some clothing boutiques, and I went into the shop.

I pushed open the door, and a bell tinkled above my head, announcing my presence. My nostrils were assaulted by the dusty smell of old books. Smiling to myself, I lifted my sunglasses onto the top of my head and started making my way around the small space.

"Be with you in just a second," a voice called out just as I began to browse the overflowing shelves.

Losing myself in the titles, covers, and blurbs, I faintly heard footsteps behind me.

"Hey, can I help?"

I turned to face quite possibly the most beautiful man I had ever seen. His light brown hair had been bleached by the sun, and the bundle of messy curls made my fingers itch to tangle them among the chaotic strands. The man's hazel eyes regarded both me and the slim book in my hand. His tall, lean figure was clad in skinny jeans, with an open, oversized shirt over a t-shirt and well-worn biker boots. He looked a little out-of-place among the surfer types I had noticed wandering around town.

"I'm just looking, thanks." I couldn't help but blush when he gave a slight smirk at the sight of the Mills & Boon book I held.

"If you're after more . . . er . . . books in that particular genre, there's a wider selection over here." He indicated a bookcase to his left.

"This? Oh, no. This isn't my type at all. I was just moving it out of the way to get at the new James Patterson."

He cocked an eyebrow and his smile grew at my obvious lie. "Yeah, okay. I'll leave you to . . . peruse." He chuckled to himself as he made his way back behind the counter.

I slammed the bright pink book down so I could grab the James Patterson, the one I'd initially been after, and walked over to pay. "I'll take this one." I thrust my card at him and waited while he ran it through. I knew it was a simple misunderstanding, but it rubbed me the wrong way. Why couldn't I just accept that he thought I wanted the Mills & Boon book? It was an easy mistake to make, I guess.

"Are you sure you don't want the other one, too? It seems a bit more . . . your style." He looked me up and down, taking in my denim shorts, skimpy vest top, and flip-flops.

His scrutiny made me nervous. I took a deep breath and ran my fingers through my hair to calm myself. "What would you know about my 'style'?" I demanded, snatching the book out of his hand and clutching it to me, almost as if it were a security blanket.

I moved to retrieve my card, but he whipped it just out of my reach.

"I've worked here for at least five years, and in that time, I've become very good at reading people. You are definitely steamy romance material, with your pretty hair and . . ." He indicated my clothes and swallowed, ". . . and your skimpy clothes."

"Well, it just goes to show that you're not as good as you thought, then. Please give me back my card." I held out my hand.

Once he'd returned the piece of plastic, I spun on my heel and walked out. I planned to read my book slowly, because I wasn't going to go back there.

§ø∂

I was still fuming when I got back to the car. Erica was sitting in the driver's seat, tapping away on her phone.

"*There* you are. I was about to send out a search party. Have fun?"

I flopped into the passenger seat with a non-committal grunt.

"That good, huh?" She gave me a sideways glance, and then pulled out of the car park.

I stared out the window, book clutched in my hand. How bloody dare he presume I were some bimbo who couldn't appreciate a 'real' book just because of my appearance? I was half-tempted to get Erica to take me back so I could yell at him, but I *really* didn't want to see him again.

We arrived at the house, and I immediately fell in love with it. It was small; there wasn't anything special about it in particular, but to me, it was perfect. The wide windows, the beachfront location, and its cosy feel made me relax just looking at it. I could already picture myself sitting on the wrap-around porch in the evenings with a glass of wine, a good book, and my headphones. I climbed out of the car and stretched.

"I'm starving. Can we go and get settled?" Erica asked, climbing out herself with a yawn.

"It's the sea air. I bet you'll be asleep by ten tonight." I sniggered while we emptied the car and walked along the gravel drive to the house.

"That would be nice. I'm usually up til two or three o'clock in the morning."

I wasn't surprised. Erica was the type of woman who went to bed late and got up early, yet still looked amazing. In all honesty, I *should* hate her. "Be careful; that candle you've lit at both ends going to burn away completely one day," I warned her while she unlocked the front door.

సౌ౭

After eating a glorious dinner and fattening desert, we explored the little house to decide which rooms to claim for our own. I decided on the back bedroom, which overlooked the ocean.

It didn't have an en suite like Erica's, but that didn't bother me. What I cared about was the view. I quickly unpacked my case, put everything away, and then made up the bed with the linens provided.

Once everything was done, I sat on the cushioned window seat and looked out over the darkening beach. I didn't feel tired; in fact, I had never felt so relaxed. Just as I pulled on a cardigan to go for a walk, my phone rang. It was Marcus, so I sat back down to speak to him.

Our phone call was the usual transfer of pleasantries and uncomfortable chit-chat. He had never been verbose over the phone, but in the last couple of years, he had grown steadily worse. He just asked if there was anything I would need when I got back home. I knew it was his way of letting me know he was thinking about me, but sometimes I wished he would just say what he meant. Was it so hard to tell me he missed me?

Fifteen minutes later, I was walking along the sand barefoot, but I continued to think about my conversation with Marcus. I couldn't concentrate on the view and the quiet, so I returned to the house and found Erica sitting on the back porch with a bottle of wine and two glasses.

"Expecting company?" I asked, sitting on the bench next to her.

"I am indeed. I have the most annoying friend; she doesn't stop talk — Ouch!" She broke off and started laughing when I gave her a rather pathetic thump on the arm.

I took the proffered glass and sipped the chilled liquid. "Thanks for this — all of this." I couldn't drag my eyes away from the ocean as I spoke.

"Thanks for coming with me, Miss Ava Jones."

I smiled at Erica, and our conversation dwindled into silence while we sat and watched the waves. When I'd finished my drink, I stood, ready to head to bed.

"Oh, the boiler's broken," Erica told me, "so there's no hot water for a shower. The landlady's nephew is popping over in the morning to try and fix it."

I nodded my understanding and went inside.

# Chapter 3

## Act One, Scene Three

Morning arrived, along with slight disorientation and a backache. I lay in the too-soft bed, staring at the ceiling while I tried to work out where I was. It wasn't until I sat up, looked out of the window, and saw the gorgeous view that I remembered. Walking over to the large window, I spent several minutes just looking out at the sea before I pulled on my running gear and headed outside.

I was out running for a good couple of hours, music pumping in time with the beat of my feet on the sand. Although I missed running with the dogs, I relished having time to myself to think. When I grew tired, I began to walk back to the house to stretch out and cool down my muscles while still enjoying the warm sea air.

Approaching the house, I could see a dark blue van parked in the wide driveway next to Erica's car, which reminded me that the boiler was being repaired.

"Hi, honey, I'm home!" I called out, walking into the kitchen to grab a bottle of water from the fridge. There was no response, but I could hear Erica's voice speaking to someone upstairs. I gulped down some of the water and headed up to see if I would be able to take a shower yet.

"So, whenever the hot water doesn't come on, you'll need to press and hold this button for a few seconds. I'll have a word with Aunty May about getting it replaced altogether," a muffled voice from the airing cupboard explained while Erica hovered.

I could see a pair of legs and an appealing backside clad in combat trousers, which led to feet encased in heavy work boots.

"That's great. At least we can have a shower now." Erica spotted me when I reached the top of the stairs and grinned. "Oh, hey, Ava. Morgan's just finished up with the boiler. It's not fixed, but we can have a shower, at least."

The man withdrew himself from the cupboard and rose to his full height. To my chagrin, it was the arrogant arse from the bookshop. He once again smirked openly while he looked me up and down, taking in my sweaty and dishevelled clothes and hair. It *would* be him; of course it would.

"Great; I could do with a shower after my run." I spoke icily, ignoring him when walked past them both, and closed my bedroom door behind me. I could hear Erica apologising on my behalf, which pissed me off even more.

Erica pounced as soon as I emerged, freshly washed, dried, and dressed, to make myself some toast and a cup of tea. "What the hell was that all about?"

"What was what?"

"Why were you so rude to Morgan?" She glared at me. "He was checking you out."

"I don't care if he was checking me out or not. That was the guy from the bookshop." I was starting to feel a little defensive under her unwavering examination.

"From the . . ? Oh, yesterday when you got all arsy over a case of absolutely nothing?"

Sympathy wasn't one of Erica's strong points. When I'd told her what had happened, she'd laughed and said that I should just forget about it.

"So you say. Is it so wrong to take offence when someone judges me just because of how I look? Especially an arrogant man I've never met before?" I huffed and crossed my arms, which only made her laugh at me.

"Ava, I love you dearly, but you need to chill. I'm sure Morgan didn't mean anything by it."

"Erica, stop. He pissed me off, and I just don't like him. Can we drop it?"

"But he's *gorgeous!*"

"He could be Johnny bloody Depp; he's still an arse. Is he going to need to come over again?"

"Probably not."

I let out a sigh of relief.

"Good. But if he does, give me fair warning so I can make sure I'm somewhere else."

"Whatever." She rolled her eyes at my request but didn't push further. "What have you planned for the rest of the day?"

"Absolutely nothing." I grinned. "I'm going to sit on the porch and enjoy the glorious weather with my book and an endless supply of tea and biscuits."

"Don't read too fast, otherwise you'll have to go and buy another," Erica teased before she sauntered out of the kitchen.

I stuck my tongue out at her retreating back.

"I saw that, child!"

I'd been immersed in the world of Alex Cross for almost three hours when Erica tapped me on the shoulder to ask if I wanted to join her for a walk on the beach. Declining with a shake of my head, I stood up from the comfortable wicker chair and went inside to make a fresh drink. Erica skipped down the steps that led onto the sand while I watched from the window.

"Hello? Anyone home?" a voice called out.

I turned round just in time to see Morgan walk into the kitchen uninvited. *Wonderful.*

His voice turned from friendly to ice-cold in a split second when he saw me. "Oh, hi."

I didn't return the greeting, preferring to stand and wait for him to explain his presence.

"I think I left a couple of tools up by the boiler. Is it okay if I go up and check?" His tone suggested that he didn't care whether he had my permission or not.

I was tempted to refuse, but I wanted him gone as fast as possible.

"Go ahead." I picked up my cup, went back out to my seat, and pretended to read. It was impossible to concentrate, knowing he was upstairs alone. The situation made me too uncomfortable. What if he decided to get nosey and go for a look around?

I'd just decided to go up and check on him when he walked out onto the porch, tools in hand.

"Found them." Morgan hovered in the doorway that led from the kitchen, and I couldn't help admiring his tall form again. His combat trousers hung low on his narrow hips, while his tight black t-shirt hugged the planes of his chest and upper arms.

Dragging my eyes away from him was difficult, but I managed it, my face hot with embarrassment.

"Oh, good," I replied. Why wasn't he leaving? I glanced at him before darting my eyes back to my book.

"I just . . . er . . . I wanted . . ." he stammered. If I hadn't disliked him so much, I would have found his struggle to find the right words endearing.

"You wanted to what?" I snapped, looking up at his face.

That was a mistake. His hazel eyes locked onto my own, enthralling me. A fog suddenly began to build up in my frontal lobe.

"Is your sentence going to start anytime soon?" I couldn't stop the bitchy tone in my voice when I snapped out the words. The way he'd spoken to me in the bookshop was still a little too fresh, and my reaction to his looks had befuddled me. He opened his mouth to speak again but thought better of it, and he stormed away to his van without another word.

The look on Morgan's face just before he walked away from me had been stuck on a loop in my head. I didn't want to keep thinking about him, but I couldn't seem to stop. What was it about this ridiculously good-looking man that made me act like a prime bitch? I detested rudeness, and as Erica had mentioned, I was never rude to people, even when provoked as I felt I had been in the bookshop. So why did my standards fly out of the window in Morgan's presence?

I resolved not to think about him for the rest of the holiday. It wasn't as if I'd see him again once we went home, and if I were careful, I wouldn't even have to see him before we left.

I was halfway through cooking a light dinner when Erica arrived back at the house. After she dashed upstairs to freshen up, she joined me in the kitchen.

"Did you have a fun-filled afternoon?" she asked while she delved into the steak and salad I had prepared.

"Not particularly." I sat opposite her and began to eat my own food.

"Anything interesting happen?"

"Apart from forgetting to eat my biscuits, no." I felt as if I were being pumped for information. "What did you get up to?"

While Erica told me about her afternoon walking along the beach eyeing up all the surfer dudes, I found myself thinking about my encounter with Morgan again. Maybe I should go and apologise to him — be the bigger person. My eyes drifted over to the book I had almost finished. It gave me the perfect excuse to see him without resorting to blowing up the boiler.

"Earth to Ava." Erica's voice jolted me out of my thoughts.

"Sorry, spaced out for a second there," I apologized with a weak smile.

"What's wrong?"

"I need to go to the bookshop tomorrow." I indicated the book on the countertop. "I'm not looking forward to it."

"I'm not surprised. You were bang out of order this morning."

Her words made me feel like a six-year-old being told off for drawing on the walls.

"I've never seen you act like that, and I think you need to go and apologise to him. Morgan seems like a nice guy. If you gave him a chance, I think you'd quite like him." She winked at me suggestively.

"Stop trying to set me up with him. Have you forgotten about Marcus?"

Erica rolled her eyes at the mention of his name. "Sometimes, I wish both of us could."

I returned her eye roll.

"You *know* your relationship has reached its 'best before' date. Neither of you are truly happy, so why don't you get off your arse and do something about it?"

I couldn't deny what she was saying; I'd said it to myself often enough.

"We've just drifted apart. I'm sure we can get things back to how they were." I didn't believe my own words, but I would have felt guilty if I hadn't at least *attempted* to convince Erica . . . and myself. I owed it to both Marcus and myself to try and get our life back to how it had been.

# Chapter 4

# Act One, Scene Four

For almost an hour, I gave myself an internal pep talk over a frappuccino in the café opposite Morgan's bookshop. After I had put my useless mental pompoms away, I gave myself a bitch-slap for being completely ridiculous and childish. All I needed to do was stand up, put one foot in front of the other, and enter the shop. If he were there, I could apologise, buy a couple of books, and then get the hell out and continue my holiday guilt-free.

The bell tinkled when I opened the door. A furtive glance around told me that Morgan wasn't in the immediate vicinity, which gave me the chance to calm down enough to act nonchalant.

"Just a minute!" a very un-Morgan-like female voice called out.

Great; he wasn't on duty. A repeat trip was going to be in order. While I moved around the shop, I spotted a couple of books that I had been after, so I grabbed them and went to wait at the counter.

"Sorry, the bloody stockroom is a complete and utter mess." A dust-covered teenage girl appeared.

"No worries." I considered asking for Morgan, but before I even got the chance, the bell above the door tinkled. From the prickle on the back of my neck, I knew it was him.

"Hey, Gemma. Did I leave my bag here this morning?"

I was starting to worry about his mental facilities; he seemed to forget things a lot. I didn't turn to look at him while Gemma rang up my selections. My already-frazzled nerves went into overdrive when he passed behind me, closely enough that I could feel the warmth of his body. I prayed under my breath that he wouldn't notice me, even though that had been the whole purpose of my visit.

"Yeah, I found it in the stockroom, so I put it under the desk in the office." Gemma turned back to me when I handed over my card to pay. "You've got great taste in literature," she remarked while she placed everything in a bag. I grinned at her in thanks. I wondered what Morgan would think about her statement, considering our first meeting.

"Thanks." Giving her a final smile, I walked to the door. Just as I put my hand on the knob, I realised I still hadn't spoken to Morgan. His voice addressed the young girl again, and I decided to chicken out. On the plus side, there was no rudeness between us, but the lack of actual words may have been a factor.

After building myself up to talk to Morgan, I wasn't in the mood to go back to the house. Erica would no doubt question me about my trip, considering she had talked me into the whole apology in the first place. I loved her like a sister, but when I was feeling stressed in any way, she wasn't the best person to be with. So I decided take a walk along the promenade for a while and try to see a bit more of the small town.

When I'd been at school, the head teacher had always given one particular speech around exam time: "How to be alone without being lonely." He'd meant to encourage independent study, but all it achieved was to drive us insane. Still, looking back now, I could see where he had been coming from. In a room full to the brim with my friends, I often felt left out and out of my depth. Yet over the past two days in the house with Erica, I had managed to spend a lot of time on my own without *feeling* alone. That was the joy of our friendship; neither of us felt the need to live in each other's pockets every minute of the day. No doubt, we'd spend some days here together, out and about, but it wasn't a requisite for the holiday.

I'd always considered myself a city girl through and through. I'd never spent much time in the country, even when on holiday abroad, until now. Being somewhere so quiet had taken me a while to get used to, but after just a couple of days, I was struggling to imagine going back to the sounds and smells of urban life. I'd never really wanted to live anywhere other than a bustling metropolis, but after being at the spa and the beach house, I could picture me and the dogs taking a step back from the hustle and bustle to live a slower-paced life. The whole idea appealed to me more with each passing day; I just wasn't sure if I could picture living this kind of live with Marcus, and that thought made me nervous.

Walking along the promenade, I soaked up the glorious sunshine while watching families play on the sand below me. Not too far along the beach, I saw an outcrop of rocks that looked like it would be the perfect place to sit and read for a while. The discoloured surface was smooth and warm from the sun, and I soon made myself comfortable on one of the flat stones, a book in my hands and headphones on my ears. I quickly got lost in a world of corruption and intrigue woven by the words of the author; the drums and guitars playing in my ears completely muffled any sounds coming from the beach. Page after page, I was sucked further into the story while the real world dissolved around me, leaving me to follow the lead character around as if I were a cameraman on a film set.

I was so engrossed that it took me a while to register a light tapping on my shoulder. Lowering the book, I pulled off one of my headphones and squinted up at the silhouette leaning over me. *Shit.*

Morgan lowered himself to sit next to me. What was he doing here?

"Hi," was his simple greeting. He didn't even look at me, rummaging through his own bag until he pulled out a dog-eared copy of *Catch 22*.

Shrugging my shoulders, I turned my attention back to my own book and tried to immerse myself once more. However, it was impossible to concentrate with him sitting so close; we were almost touching. He could have chosen anywhere on the vast expanse of rock, but he'd sat right next to me. Why?

"I can hear you thinking."

I looked up to find him watching me with that bloody half-smile on his face. It really irritated me. "Is that why you sat here? Did you just want to wind me up?" I began to shove my book back into my bag, my hands trembling with the urge to hit him. I was shocked that after knowing him just a couple of days, I was considering risking a charge of Actual Bodily Harm whenever this man was in my vicinity.

"I sat here because this is where I always sit after a shift at the shop." He grabbed my wrist when I moved to stand. "Look, I didn't plan on winding you up; it just seems to happen."

I glared at him until he released my arm.

"It seems to be my natural reaction to you. And you bite back . . . it's obvious that you're not keen on me. Any reason in particular? You know, so I can work on my people skills. Not that they've ever failed me before."

Oh, the bloody audacity of him.

"Yeah. The fact that you're up your own arse and . . . and . . ." I scrambled for something — *anything*. My eyes fell to the book in his hands. ". . . and your reading material makes you look like a pretentious twat." I shot another glare at him before stalking back to the promenade, my good mood ruined. How could he suggest that he acted like an idiot in retaliation for how I acted towards him? It was his own fault that I didn't like him.

I was so angry that I ended up forgoing the little bus that could have taken me back to the house. Instead, I walked the whole five miles. How bloody dared Morgan joke about it being my fault that we didn't get on? Thinking about how cocksure and arrogant he was made me grind my teeth together to stop myself screaming out loud in the street. Any idea I'd had about apologising for my rudeness had flown out the window. My feet were aching from stomping around in my flip-flops, but I was still too riled up to care.

When I reached the small convenience shop at the end of our road, I popped in to pick up some provisions. Wine was a no-go; my mood called for the strongest cider I could get my hands on, accompanied by fattening chips and dip. Tonight, I was going to get shit-faced, good and proper. And Erica was joining me, whether she liked it or not.

# Chapter 5

## Act Two, Scene One

"Ava, I don't care what you want. We are going into town tonight. We will get dressed up. We will dance, drink, and maybe get chatted up. Most of all, lady, you will stop being a miserable bitch and enjoy yourself."

Erica sounded a little fed up, not that I could blame her. The last three days had consisted of me wallowing in my anger over Morgan, often muttering about him in rage. I felt bad.

"What should I wear?" I conceded. Maybe this would be just what I needed to get out of my funk.

❦

"I can see myself living somewhere like this." I blurted out when Erica linked her arm with mine to stop me swaying. Unfortunately, she was unable to prevent my words from slurring.

"Me, too. It must be a bit rubbish off-season, though."

I considered what the quiet months without tourists would be like. "I don't think it would be. It would be a nice break from the tourism madness."

We joined the end of the queue outside the area's busiest club.

"A chance to live without having to deal with strangers invading your home for three or four months," I mused while we waited to be let inside.

"I guess, but I don't think I could deal with how quiet it is." Erica's words echoed my thoughts from earlier in the week.

"It's not that quiet, in all honesty. It's just different noise." My defence of beach life took me by surprise; I'd never expected to have this kind of a reaction to somewhere so new to me.

The queue moved at a decent pace, and the bouncer was soon scrutinising us. He must have decided to ignore our near-inebriation, because he waved us through. Erica dragged me straight to the bar. While she flirted with the barman, I scanned the dark room. The dance floor was already filled with writhing bodies, and I could feel the deep bass reverberating in my chest.

"Drink up, then we dance."

I was handed a shot of something neon pink, and I knocked it back in one without questioning what it was. As soon as I'd put the glass back on the bar, Erica led me through the gyrating tourists to the dance floor.

Erica was a natural dancer, and I usually felt subpar next to her tall, slender frame. Tonight, I didn't care, thanks to the alcohol flowing through my bloodstream. Since Erica had plied me with drinks all evening, I had lost all of my inhibitions about dancing in public. I closed my eyes and began to move to the music, making a mental note to thank her in the morning once the inevitable hangover had passed.

We'd been dancing for less than ten minutes when Erica drew the attention of a surfer. He snuck in behind her and began to move with her, his hands on her waist. I grinned as she turned to face him, wrapping her arms around his neck and letting him lead. Their movements were becoming more explicit, and Erica shot me a wide smile over his shoulder. I gestured to her that I was going to the bathroom and would be back with her soon, and she nodded her response while the surfer began to nuzzle her neck.

Working my way through the heaving throng, I finally hit an empty, air-conditioned section of the club. I stood for a while, allowing my sweaty skin to cool before I continued on to the ladies'. Squeezing through the usual gaggle of gossiping women and into a cubicle was awkward, but I managed.

I emerged a few minutes later. The music had gotten faster, and there were even more people on the dance floor. Before going to find Erica, I stood and watched the masses. Just as I began to take a step, I was almost knocked to the floor.

"Shit, I'm sorry. Are you okay?" Large, warm hands gripped my upper arms to steady me.

I looked up into bright, hazel eyes that rendered me speechless and made my stomach flip.

And then I recognised them.

"You again?" Morgan let go of me like he'd been burnt.

"Yeah, it's me," I griped, hands on my hips. The tall bottle-blonde with him snorted in derision, but I ignored her.

"I didn't expect to find you somewhere like this. I took you for more of a wine bar kinda girl." Morgan cast his eyes over my low-cut dress and wet-look leggings. "I guess you're getting a kick out of slumming it."

He walked away with the blonde in tow before I managed to answer. It took every ounce of strength in me not to go charging after him and lay into him. I'd never known a single person who was able to get me so riled up just by being in the same room. Even if he didn't speak, there was something about him that caused me to raise my protective shield.

It might have been the way he looked at me with that maddening smirk on his handsome face. Whatever the reason, I made a pact with myself not to let him ruin the rest of my holiday while I glared at his retreating back.

♥♥

The next morning, I wasn't particularly surprised to find Erica's dance partner from the night before making coffee when I stumbled into the kitchen.

"Morning." His gruff voice didn't match his youthful face.

"Hi." I rummaged through my bag, trying to locate some painkillers. Although I didn't get hangovers very often, when I did, they were excruciating. The bright sunlight wasn't helping, so I pulled on my oversized sunglasses and sat at the tiny table, holding my head in my hands.

Chuckling softly, Erica's boy-toy placed a steaming mug of black coffee in front of me before heading back upstairs, whistling while he walked.

A few hours later, Erica found me on the porch, dozing in the shade on the wicker sofa. She sat in the chair next to me, her tired eyes the only indication of the night she'd had.

"How are you feeling?" she asked, trying to hide her smug, post-coital smile.

"What was that pink stuff you kept buying last night?" I sat up with caution and was happy to discover my head no longer spun.

"I have no bloody idea." A sheepish look flickered across her face. "I'm sorry about . . . er . . ." She tapped the front of her head gently, ". . . Liam. I know it's not *that* kind of holiday, but he's so pretty, and it's been so long . . ."

I started laughing at her. "Oh, shut up, you silly bint. I don't mind you bringing baby face back. Just be thankful you didn't wake me up."

The blush creeping up her neck just made me laugh even harder.

Erica floated around in her bubble of satisfaction for the rest of the day. I even caught her humming to herself while she made us a light lunch.

"I heard that there's going to be a beach party on Friday. Fancy it?" she asked once we sat down to eat.

Considering it, I found that I liked the idea. We were leaving early Sunday morning, so it would be a good last hurrah. I also assumed from the look on her face when I agreed to go that Liam would be there. Good for her; one final fling before we went home. I kind of wished I could indulge, but cheating wasn't my style.

I'd seen beach parties in films and on American television shows, and they always looked fantastic. It would be a great way to start saying goodbye to the Isle of Wight. Most things I was sad to leave behind, while other aspects I wouldn't miss at all. Just the memory of Morgan sneering at me under the strobe lights caused a flicker of my anger to resurface.

The honk of a car horn brought me back to the present, and I looked out of the window to see the man himself climbing out of his van.

# Chapter 6

## Act Two, Scene Two

"Where are you going?" Erica was a little surprised at my sudden movement as I got to my feet.

"To my room. Let me know when he's gone." I couldn't stop myself running up to my room, where I sat on the window seat and watched life on the beach. After a while, it started to get a bit stuffy, so I pushed the windows wide open. I lay my arms on the frame, and then rested my chin on them. It took me a moment to realise that the voices I heard over the sound of the wind and waves were coming from the porch below me instead of from the beach.

"We go home on Sunday, Morgan. I don't know why she reacts to you the way she does, and I don't think five days enough time to find out."

"She just seems to bring out the worst in me, and I don't know why. Normally, I'd flirt and play nice, but Ava gets under my skin, and not in a good way. All because of a simple mistake I made when we first met."

I snorted, and then panicked in case they had heard me.

"Look, if you can stop being a dick and are able to manage to talk to her in a civil manner, we're going to the party on Friday night. Even if all you do is make peace with her before we leave, it's better than nothing."

"If she'll even listen to me. I don't know if you've noticed, but that friend of yours is kind of pigheaded. I'll give it a go; what's the worst that could happen?"

Erica snorted this time. Traitorous bitch.

The rest of the week was mostly spent down on the beach with Erica. During that time, I was plagued with visions of fighting with Morgan at the beach party. Although I'd resolved to give him the chance to apologise for being a total arrogant arse, I was ready to let him know exactly what I thought of him if he managed to balls that up.

Friday arrived with the best weather we'd seen, even though it had been gorgeous the entire time we'd been there. Throughout the day, I watched while groups of people marked out a large area not only for the party itself, but also for the bonfire that would be lit just before sunset. I was finally getting my movie beach scene.

The party was due to start by mid-afternoon, and already at least a dozen barbeques had been set up. Erica had driven to the big supermarket in town to stock up on cider for the day. Why she'd picked cider, I had no idea. I'd never seen her touch the stuff, but there were currently three cases sitting in the bath, together with six of the ten bags of ice she'd also bought. I could only assume the nearest off-licences were running a bit dry thanks to the party. Luckily, party central was pretty much on our doorstep, which meant we didn't have to lug all thirty-six bottles down onto the sand.

Knowing that Morgan was going to be there had influenced my decision on what to wear. It annoyed the hell out of me that he had that much of an effect on me, but I didn't want him to think I was a snooty cow. I kept it simple and safe, electing to wear a black bikini under denim shorts and a loose linen top. Since I would only be walking from the beach to the house, I chose to remain barefoot. Erica seemed to have the same idea and wore a similar outfit, except her long legs were hidden under a sarong, and she'd decided against a top over her blood-red bikini.

"You looking forward to this?" she asked while we ate a light sandwich before joining the growing crowd on the beach.

"I am, although I'm getting a little bit sad, knowing we've got to go back home in just two days." The temptation to stay in this idyllic little town was strong, even if just for a short while longer. Going home and settling back into my non-life wasn't appealing. I was only looking forward to being with the dogs again; I had missed my babies like crazy, but I was sad to realise they were the only thing I *had* missed.

"Hey, earth to Ava."

I blinked a couple of times and noticed that Erica was waving her hand in front of my face.

"You in there?"

"Sorry, yeah. I was just working out how to avoid real life for a while longer."

"Oh, honey." She took my hands in her own. "What are you trying to avoid?"

I knew that she already knew the answer to that question and had done for a long time, but it was finally time for me to admit it out loud.

"Marcus." Verbalising it didn't hurt as much as I'd expected it to. "I hate to admit this, but you were right. I don't think either of us is happy. We're just each other's habit, and our relationship's been stale for a long time. I just hope he understands and doesn't think I'm ending things because I've met someone out here."

"Let him think what he wants. It's not as if you're going to move someone in five minutes after he moves out."

"Oh, God! We'd have to sell and then divide everything we own. And the dogs!" I started to hyperventilate at the thought of not only losing my home, but also my babies. Marcus loved them, too, but I was the one who took them running and fed them. I was the one they snuggled up to every evening. Marcus tended to only help with baths and trips to the vet.

"I can't lose them, Erica. I couldn't cope if things got nasty and he took my babies away."

Erica pulled me into her arms and rubbed soothing circles on my back while I cried. "Shhh. It'll be okay. Let's just get this weekend dealt with, and then we can tackle Marcus together. I won't let you handle this alone, I promise."

I looked into her eyes, which flashed with fierce loyalty. "I bloody love you." I pulled her into another hug. "Thank you for everything."

❧❧

The sand was warm against my feet while I walked from the house to join the party. I'd gotten over my fit of the weepies, washed the blotches from my face with cool water, and then applied minimal makeup to ensure I looked somewhat human. With a final fluff of my lose hair, I felt ready to face the world — and Morgan.

With an ice-cold bottle of cider slowly warming in my hand, I wandered around, looking for Erica. I found her with Liam and his friends, who were manning one of the barbeques. The aromas hit me, making my stomach rumble and my mouth water. I grabbed a burger, slapped it in a bun with a touch of salad, and smothered it in spicy relish, before sitting with Erica to eat.

Listening to the many conversations going on around me without joining in, I continued to think about Marcus and how he was going to respond to my decision when I got home. I'd ignored the situation for so long, but now that I'd made my final choice, I just wanted it over and done with.

All the talk about finding the perfect wave and overuse of the word 'dude' was beginning to bore me, so I told Erica I was going to get another drink and mingle some. I walked away before she had the chance to respond. The house was so cool; I sat down to enjoy it for a while, sipping at my fresh drink. After a while, I decided to go see what else was happening at the party. I grabbed my sunglasses and walked back out into the heat.

"Ava?" Morgan jogged up the stairs to meet me. "Could I have a word with you?"

# Chapter 7

## Act Two, Scene Three

We walked together towards the pier that marked the end of the party area. The silence between us was uncomfortable, but I was damned if I was going to break it first. I just trudged alongside him, watching him out of the corner of my eye. It was a bit of a struggle not to stop and blatantly stare at his body, which he'd dressed in black board shorts and nothing else. The well-defined muscles that were usually hidden by a shirt were now on display, and I found them distracting. My mouth began to water again, but not from hunger. Still, I waited for him to speak.

"You didn't seem very surprised to see me," he began.

It wasn't the conversation starter I'd expected. "Well, you live in the area. I knew there was a possibility that you'd be at the party."

"That's not what I meant, and you know it. You heard Erica and me talking the other day. I heard your little snort of derision."

I blushed. "Yeah, about that . . ."

He held up his hand to stop me. "It's fine. It makes this a little easier."

We reached the very edge of the party area and stopped. I turned to look at the vast expanse of water.

"What are you thinking about?" he asked while he watched my face with those amazing eyes of his.

"I just realised that I've been here for almost ten days, and I haven't been swimming once." I hadn't planned on telling him that.

"That's no good." He took two steps towards the water, turned back to me, and held out his hand.

Giving into the impulse, I quickly removed my shorts, top, and sunglasses. Dropping them in a pile on the sand, I tentatively took his hand, allowing him to lead me to the water's edge.

Without any warning and still holding onto my hand, Morgan suddenly charged into the water at full speed, dragging me behind him, my legs working without me realising it until I hit the water.

"What the hell did you do that for?" I spluttered, wiping my wet hair off my face and checking that my bikini top hadn't malfunctioned when we'd hit the water.

"It's the best way to acclimatise, especially on a day like today."

"Well, you could have warned me," I huffed while I struggled to tie my hair into a lopsided topknot.

"But would you have done it if I had?"

"Probably not, but still . . ."

"*But still,* nothing."

Remaining upright and treading water, I watched him float on his back. This time, the silence wasn't uncomfortable. I closed my eyes, leaned back, and allowed the water to support me.

"Although you already know what I want to say, I think I should say it anyway."

I stayed quiet, listening to his voice. He took a deep breath. When he began to speak again, I opened my eyes to look at him.

He was still on his back: arms spread, eyes closed, and a troubled look on his face. "That day in the bookshop . . . I don't know why I acted like that." He allowed his legs to drop back into the water, bringing him upright to face me. I was surprised to see how nervous he appeared when he finally opened his eyes to look at me.

"Morgan, you don't need to do this right now," I tried to reassure him, for some unknown reason. I hated him . . . didn't I?

"Yes, I do. If we get out of the water, you'll find somewhere else to be: somewhere, anywhere, nowhere near me."

He wasn't wrong. I had considered finding Erica as soon as we hit dry sand; I just needed to get out of the water first.

"I made an assumption about you that day. It's high season; not many young women who look the way you do come into the shop, much less to buy the latest crime bestseller."

"It wasn't you guessing I read chick lit that offended me. I've had that a lot. It was the way you assumed you knew me simply because I looked like other women my age you'd dealt with. You were so confident and cocky, and that pissed me off more than the judgement you made."

"I can see that now. I did plan to apologise the next day when we were on the porch, but you were being a snippy cow. It made me see red. I left before I said something I would have regretted."

"I guess I owe you an apology, too." It was a little late to feel guilty for being such a bitch to him, but at least we were making our peace with each other. I was going home in a couple of days, and now I would be able to look back without any regrets.

"And I guess we'd best be getting out of the water; your lips are starting to turn blue." He grabbed my hand again and began to swim towards the sand, pulling me along with him.

Since I hadn't been expecting to go swimming, I didn't have a towel with me, so I had to walk back in just my bikini, allowing the sun to dry my skin. I felt a little self-conscious, but considering there was a slew of bikini clad bodies around me, I tried not to let it bother me too much.

"Ava!"

I turned to find Erica jogging over to Morgan and me like a Baywatch extra.

"Where the hell have you been?"

"I went for a swim . . . with Morgan." I tried not to laugh at the way Erica looked at the pair of us, mouth opening and closing like a fish out of water.

"With . . . *what?* I thought you hated him." Cue mental bitch-slap.

Luckily, Morgan took it well. "She did, but I spiked her drink, carried her off into the sea, and wouldn't let her go until she agreed to have my children. In fact, that's where we're headed right now; we need get started on that football team." Without giving Erica a chance to respond, he grabbed my hand and stalked up to the house, only slowing to grab a fresh beer.

Morgan slammed the kitchen door closed behind us, and I collapsed in a heap of full-on giggles.

"You bloody idiot! Why did you say that to her?" I ran upstairs to grab another bottle of cider from the bath and took a large gulp to get rid of the saltwater tainting my mouth.

"Oh, come on. You have to admit that was funny." He was laughing so hard that tears were running down his face, drawing my eyes to the blonde stubble that emphasised his strong jaw line.

I couldn't stop my smile getting wider, but there was no way on God's green earth that I was going to admit out loud that it *was* funny. "Poor Erica."

That set him off laughing again.

"Even worse, poor you . . ."

His laughter stopped dead. "Why poor me?"

I smiled the sweetest smile I could muster. "Well, after telling Erica we were coming inside to get started on making babies, how's it going to look when I walk outside after we've been in here for less than five minutes?"

I pulled my shorts on, gave Morgan a wide smile, and walked back out into the sunshine, leaving my words hanging in the air and him open mouthed like a goldfish. I giggled to myself when my feet hit the sand. Now that we were getting on, I enjoyed teasing him.

# Chapter 8

## Act Three, Scene One

It was weird driving through the city on the way back home. The weather was still warm, but it felt different. The sounds around me were the hardest to readjust to. I had only just gotten used to *not* hearing them, and now they felt almost oppressive in their unrelenting consistency. When Erica pulled up outside the house, I was tempted to ask her to come in with me, not quite wanting to face reality. Instead, I put on my big girl panties. Even though it petrified me, I needed to get started on the changes that I needed to make. I wasn't sure how Marcus would react to me telling him that I felt we weren't working, but I had to make him understand that it would be better for us both. I just hoped we could be civil and reach a compromise about how to part.

When I finally summoned the courage to let myself in, I was almost suffocated when all three dogs fought to get to me first. After I'd managed to calm them down with treats and lots of fussing, I walked through the house in search of Marcus. There was no sign of him, which both relieved and disappointed me. He'd known when I would be getting back, yet he hadn't been able to bring himself to miss just one week of football.

I pottered around for a while, unpacking my bag and shoving clothes into the washing machine, and then cuddled with the dogs. After awhile, I began to get restless and started going over in my head when and how to start the discussion about ending our relationship. Flicking on the TV, I looked at it without really seeing what was happening on the screen. I must have fallen asleep, because it had gotten dark outside by the time Marcus gently shook me awake, the smell of beer enveloping him.

"Jesus, Marcus. What time is it? Why didn't you wake me earlier?" I sat up, my head feeling as though it was full of cotton wool.

"I've only just got back myself." He sounded very drunk and a little sad.

Rubbing my hands over my face, I walked into the kitchen to make a strong coffee for Marcus and a cup of tea for myself. "How did the game go?" I asked, wanting some indication of why he'd been out late drinking.

"We lost, just." So, a drowning of sorrows it was, then.

I glanced at the clock before walking back to where he sat slouched on the sofa.

"You went for a few drinks to commiserate?"

He nodded, and I handed him his drink.

I could feel my anger building. "So why are you only just getting home at ten to midnight?"

"We just got a bit carried away. A few games of pool, darts . . . you know how it is with the lads."

"No, I really don't, Marcus."

He looked shocked at my answer, which caused my irrational anger to rush to the surface.

"Look, I don't have a problem with football taking you out of the house two or three times a week; I never have. But I *do* have a problem with you not being here when I get home after being away for so long. It makes me feel like an afterthought, and to make matters worse, I didn't even get a text or a quick call to see if I got home in one piece. Great way to make me feel missed; thanks a lot, Marcus." I drained my tea and went to put the empty cup in the kitchen before I gave into the urge to hurl it at his head.

"I did miss you, Ava. It's just been . . . different around here without you."

"*Different?* Oh, thank you very much; that sounds simply wonderful. Next, you'll tell me it was nice and quiet while I was gone."

He didn't say anything, and I took a few deep breaths to calm myself down.

"What are you trying to avoid telling me, Marcus?" The anger I was still feeling was now tinged with a touch of guilt. I couldn't deny that I was relieved not to be the one to initiate this conversation.

Marcus paced the short length of the living room, swaying slightly. He seemed to be really thinking about my question, which made me realise there was only one possible outcome to this talk. Even though I had resigned myself to this, I just hadn't expected the break to happen quite so soon after my return.

"Ava, I've loved you for so long, but I don't think I was ever *in love* with you — or you with me."

I wanted to dispute his words somehow, but now was the time for complete honesty. "Are we horrible people, tying each other down for all this time?" I didn't even attempt to wipe away the tears that streamed down my face. No matter how far apart we had drifted, I didn't want Marcus to hate me.

"Not at all. We just got comfortable, I guess." He sat next to me and took my shaking hands in his, enveloping them with his warmth. "I like to think we were mostly happy, even if we grew distant over the last couple years."

I nodded in agreement. "Yeah, it was mostly good."

Marcus smiled sadly at me.

"So, what now?" I was starting to get a little scared at what his answer might be and how it would affect the future.

"That's one of the reasons I was out so late tonight. I think the best thing for now would be for me to go and stay with one of the lads. Do you . . . do you think there's a chance you'd be able to buy my share of the house and save us from selling completely?"

"I have no idea. I'd have to work it out." I felt a glimmer of hope that I might be able to stay in the house if I could just manage to find the money. Marcus was right; it would be better than selling. If we had to sell, we'd lose a chunk of money to fees and legal costs, and then we might not be able to afford separate places to live.

"Look into it. I know how much you love this house. It always was more yours than it was ever mine; same with the dogs."

My heart lurched at his words, yet I couldn't help feel relief wash over me at the thought of not having to fight with him over everything.

"I can't take them away from you, but I won't sacrifice everything." His voice was soft.

I threw my arms around him, thanking him for being so thoughtful. From that moment, I knew we were going to be okay. Too many of our friends ended things in a big ball of nasty, particularly when kids were involved.

"Marcus, I want you to know I do love you — I always have."

He smiled and thumbed away my tears before kissing my forehead and heading up to spend the night in the spare room.

# Chapter 9

## Act Three, Scene Two

"What's happening with the house, then?" Erica asked while she helped me separate Marcus's CDs and DVDs from mine.

"I don't know yet. Every time I try to work it out, I can't see how I can afford to buy him out. He's said he can wait for a while, but he's going to want to get a new place eventually, so I need to give him an answer pretty soon."

"Is selling up an option?"

"At the moment, I think it may end up being the only option." I couldn't think of anything I wanted to do less.

"You know I could hel-"

I cut her off as soon as I realised what she was going to say. "No. There's no way I can let you do that, Erica. As much as I appreciate the offer, I need to work this out for myself."

She just shrugged her shoulders, not offended by my refusal. Nothing ever seemed to ruffle her feathers, and for that, I was grateful. "You'll find a way; I know you will." She glanced at the clock on the wall. "Oh, I have to go. I have a date," she told me with a grin.

"Oh? Why am I just hearing about this now?"

"Because I only confirmed it twenty minutes ago."

"Well, tell me all about him."

"I don't need to; you've already met him."

"I have? When?" I couldn't remember being introduced to any prospective dates since we'd been back.

"You met Liam last week. It turns out he lives locally, so we're going out for dinner now he's back from Ryde."

"Liam? Oh, baby face." Was that a hint of a blush on my best friend's cheeks? "I thought that was just a fling — a holiday romance."

"So did I, until he sent me a text yesterday. That boy does good sexting." She fanned herself while we walked to the door. "Thought I'd give him another go. In every sense of the word."

I wished her luck and gave her a hug before watching her walk along the path to the street. Then taking a deep breath, I went back to the piles of junk in the living room.

ထဲ

Marcus had been true to his word and moved into a friend's spare room. He'd spent the past week sorting out storage space in the loft and garage at his parents' house, and he was coming to collect some boxes at the weekend. Due to the calm and civil manner in which we'd parted ways, I didn't feel the need to leave the house while he was around to avoid seeing him. Erica couldn't understand and thought it was weird that our relationship hadn't imploded in a big ball of tears, snot, and shattered china. That was the way her relationships tended to end, not that I blamed her. If I had gone through what she had with Joey, I would find it hard to trust men, too. I just hoped Liam didn't screw her over too much, even though I was happy that she was willing to give him a chance.

Over the following fortnight, I stressed myself out about the house to the point where I felt physically sick. I didn't want to leave my home. I adored living there, but I was unable to see any other way round the situation.

Marcus hadn't hassled me once since he'd moved out; if it had been me, I would have been on his case. As our time apart grew longer, the date of the next mortgage payment grew closer, and I wound myself up even more while I began to resign myself to the actuality of moving out.

Three days before the mortgage payment was due, Marcus called to ask if he could pop over after work to talk. I ended the call in full panic mode and started pacing around the house, scaring the dogs and yelling at them when they thought they were going for a run. Once they had crawled into their beds, I was on my knees hugging them and apologising. The wall finally collapsed, and the tears spilled fast and furious.

Marcus would be right to insist that we sell up and split the money so that we could go our separate ways once and for all. Deep down, I knew it would be the best thing for both of us, but it still broke my heart to know I'd no longer be able to call this place my home.

To make it up to the dogs, I took them for an extra-long run around the park before I took a shower. While I was waiting for Marcus to show up, I even had a quick look online at small houses in the area, but not knowing how much money we'd make on the sale made it hard to do proper research.

I sat on the sofa, cradling a cold cup of tea and staring into space, until I heard the doorbell ring. Fighting my way through the excited dogs, I opened the door to let Marcus in.

"Sorry to say this, but you look rough, Ava." He gave me a kiss on the cheek. "I hope you haven't been stressing yourself out about the house."

My reaction told him more than any words could have: I started crying again. He wrapped me in his arms and hugged me tight. I let him lead me into the living room, where he deposited me on the sofa before disappearing into the kitchen. I managed to pull myself together just as he returned with a fresh cup of hot, steaming tea for me.

I gave him a watery smile of thanks when he sat down next to me. "It's got to be done hasn't it?" I asked him, not needing to explain myself further.

"I think so. I'm so sorry."

"It's not your fault. I tried so hard to make it work financially, but I just couldn't."

"I know, but we need to move on. I may love you, but we can't be tied to each other like this for much longer. Plus, Dave's getting fed up with having me in his spare room."

"I understand. I've got the day off tomorrow; I'll contact some local estate agents and get the ball rolling."

"Are you sure? I can contact some while I'm at work. I know it's going to be hard for you."

I hugged Marcus again and reassured that him I would be fine and that if I needed him, I'd let him know. Later that evening, I lay in bed, unable to sleep. Staring at the ceiling, I wondered where circumstances were going to lead me next. Out of nowhere, Morgan's face floated unbidden in front of my eyes. I wished I was back on the Isle of Wight, away from the mess my life had become.

The fleeting idea of moving out there crossed my mind before I pushed it away, dismissing it as ridiculous and impossible. There was no way I could completely uproot my life because of one almost-blissful holiday on the beach.

# Chapter 10

# Act Three, Scene Three

Summer was ending, and the house had been on the market for almost two weeks. Both Marcus and I had been surprised at the valuation and the speed of the process. There had been a little interest, but no views as yet. Diane, the estate agent, had said not to worry since many people were still recovering from their holidays. I wasn't too worried; it meant I could stay in the house longer. Even so, it was starting to look empty. I had been packing things away, and the bigger furniture neither of us wanted had been sold.

Erica and I still went on our weekly "date." Sometimes Liam joined us, but not always. Neither of them would admit they were a couple, even though I knew that Erica was spending more time at his place than at her own. She had started using the fated "we" when talking about things she'd done over the weekend or on a day off. I teased her mercilessly, but she knew I was happy for her. Of all the people I knew, she deserved happiness the most. She wasn't a big believer in a man making a woman happy, and I didn't blame her after the whole Joey debacle, but she was the kind of person who was made to love someone, and Liam seemed to relish and return her affections.

My life plodded along the same as ever. I went to work, ran with the dogs, and ate crappy food in the evenings. It still wasn't really a life that was worth living. I was merely existing, something both Erica and Marcus picked up on.

"Ava, lovely, you need to go out more," Erica told me when we left the pub after our meal, more than a little tipsy from the wine we'd had.

"I'm out now," I hedged

"That is *not* what I meant, and you know it!"

"Erica, I'm in the process of selling the house I love. I haven't really been in the mood to party."

"I know, honey, but you still need to have a life. I understand that this whole thing hurts like hell, but you need to stop allowing it to dictate your choices."

After I had climbed into bed that night, I thought about what Erica had said. I *did* need to make more of an effort to live my life. Did I still want to do it the same way and in the same place? Maybe I could use selling the house as an opportunity to make a complete life overhaul. For the first time, I went to sleep with a smile on my face.

The following two weeks were a flurry of viewings while I looked for somewhere to live once the house was sold. My efforts were half-hearted, since I couldn't decide where I wanted to go now that I was faced with the chance to become whatever I wanted.

I carried on with my regular routine in between having to escort strangers around my house and listening to them talk about what changes they would make. It got to me so much that I asked the estate agent to take over the viewings. When I got the phone call from Marcus telling me that an offer for the full asking price had been made, I broke down. It was real. I had to leave — *soon* — but I had nowhere to go.

Ramping up my own property search once Marcus and I accepted the offer, I still was hindered by the fact that nothing appealed to me.

"You're being too picky," Erica scolded me while we sat in my almost-empty kitchen.

I clicked the mouse to load yet another page of empty properties that I had no interest in. "I can't help it if I have a problem with moving from a three-bed house to a one- or two-bed flat," I snapped back at her, my frustration bubbling to the surface.

"Ava. Calm down."

I turned to look at her. "I'm sorry; I know I'm being a total bitch, but I can't seem to stop myself. I'm running out of time to find somewhere half-decent to live, and all I can think about is jogging along the beach." It was almost becoming an obsession.

"That holiday really affected you, didn't it?"

I closed my laptop with a soft click and took a sip of my cooling tea while I tried work out how to verbalise exactly how much those ten days had altered my outlook.

"I have never felt so at home and at peace than I did in that house; more than even here." I indicated the walls around us. "It was so warm and just . . . just . . ." It was a relief to finally be able to admit what I'd felt since leaving the Isle of Wight.

"I think I know what you're trying to say. Why don't you look into going back? You did say that you'd enjoy living somewhere like that."

I didn't speak, but I considered her words.

I stopped running and fought to catch my breath while the dogs chased each other through the damp grass. The sun was starting to set, and there were very few other people in the park. Whistling for the dogs, I clipped their leads on and began to walk back home. The last person I would have expected to find waiting on my doorstep was Liam.

"Liam, hi." My voice didn't hide my surprise.

"Hey, Ava. Sorry to drop in on you like this. Can I have a quick word?"

I assumed he was fishing for information about Erica, so I invited him inside. He followed me into the kitchen and waited quietly while I fed the dogs and freshened up their water.

"What do you want to know about her?" I blurted out once I had made us both a drink.

"I'm not here about Erica — just because of her."

Oh, shit.

He paused as if he were attempting to organise his thoughts. "She mentioned this morning how much you loved being on the Isle of Wight."

"No offence, but it's not any of your business." I hated how snippy I was being lately.

"I know it isn't, but I made some calls anyway. I hope you don't get mad." Liam looked at me, his eyes showing how nervous he was.

I simply waved my hand for him to continue.

"Well, I spoke to Morgan, and his aunty May has to sell the house because she can't cope with the upkeep anymore. It needs a fair bit of work, so she's not asking for the full value. Just thought you might be interested." He didn't seem to notice the way my breath hitched at the sound of Morgan's name.

When he smiled and stood to leave before I'd managed to get my brain in gear, I stopped staring at him and said, "Thank you, Liam. That was very sweet of you to do that for me."

"Any time. Now, I'd best get going; I'm meeting Erica for dinner."

# Chapter 11

## Act Four, Scene One

For several days following Liam's visit, I was assaulted by visions of sandy beaches and hazel eyes. I'd managed to stop thinking about Morgan and was thankful we'd parted company as friends, but Liam just mentioning his name had caused every single memory of him to cloud my vision whenever I tried to concentrate on anything else.

Even when I'd disliked Morgan, I had been able to admit to myself that I was attracted to him. He was gorgeous, and once we'd made amends, I'd discovered he was great company, too. After our swim, we'd sat together for the rest of the party talking, laughing, and drinking. There had been so much drinking. It was only now that I realised that I'd wanted more than drinking; I'd wanted to be kissed, and because of this, I couldn't stop thinking about the beach house being up for sale. Could I uproot myself to follow a pipe dream?

"Yes, you can," Erica insisted when she called me in response to the text I had sent her.

"But . . ." I'd already run out of excuses and couldn't even finish the sentence.

"Look. Just try it. If it doesn't work, rent the place out and move back here."

"You make it sound so easy." I was more than a little tempted.

"That's because it *is* easy. You're the one who's making it into such a huge issue." She sounded almost fed up with me.

"That might be because I'm a little nervous about jacking in my job and moving away from everyone and everything I know on a whim to somewhere I've been to just once for a mere ten days."

"If you're that unsure or worried, why don't you talk to Marcus about it? He's neutral enough to be honest with you." Erica ended the call after instructing me to think about it.

She was right, as usual. Marcus was very level-headed and would be honest with me. I resolved to talk to him when he came over at the weekend to collect the rest of his things.

৵৶

Marcus had loaded the last of his belongings into his car. We'd decided on which furniture would be kept or sold once the sale of the house was finalised, and then it was time for me to confess my secrets to him. I flitted around the kitchen, making us both a drink.

"Ava, you've been dithering ever since I got here. What's on your mind?" He knew me far too well.

I took a deep breath and told him all about the Isle of Wight, minus Morgan, before asking him what he thought I should do.

"It sounds to me as though you've already made up your mind but you want someone to reassure you that it's the right thing to do. No one can do that for you, Ava." Marcus looked me in the eye. "Have you got anything keeping you here that you can't take with you? Is there anyone here who wouldn't visit you if you did move?"

I shook my head.

"Well then, I think you already know what you're going to do." He kissed the top of my head, drained his cup, and left to go sort out his new flat.

I sat down to type up a resignation letter while I phoned Erica so that Liam could give me the contact details for the beach house.

�❧

I was amazed at the speed at which everything moved once the ball got rolling. Not only was the sale on the house pretty much complete and my stuff packed up, the beach house was almost mine. I felt like a walking cliché when I told Erica it was like a weight had been lifted off my shoulders as soon as I started doing something *I* wanted to do rather than what others wanted or expected me to do.

Time couldn't move fast enough for me. With one week of my notice left at work, I'd been casually looking online at jobs in and around the area, but nothing had caught my eye. Since I had worked out that I could take up to six weeks before money would start getting tight, I wasn't too worried yet.

Although I was hoping for a complete career change, I didn't know what I wanted to change it to. Knowing I could always get something temporary to tide me over while I still looked for the right thing, I tried not to stress over it. I knew there were always options out there. More than anything, I just wanted to move now that I had made the commitment.

It was going to be hard leaving Erica and my other friends, but I'd been made to promise to hold a housewarming party once I'd settled in. No one cared that the summer was pretty much over; I would have a house on the beach, and everyone would be welcome.

The day I loaded my things into a van was a little bittersweet. I wouldn't ever again set foot in the house I had called home for so long, but I *was* taking the first steps to a brand new life.

I climbed into Erica's car. The dogs were curled up on the back seat, watching me with worried, confused eyes. They soon settled down when we started driving, all of our belongings following behind us in a beaten-up old transit. Catching its reflection in the car mirror, I realized that it reminded me of a certain handyman's van, covered in sand from the beach.

# Chapter 12

## Act Four, Scene Two

Just as I'd expected, the dogs adored the beach. Once we'd pulled up outside the house on moving day, all three of them had dashed out onto the sand, unsure where to explore first.

Within our first week, they'd put me through my paces on our twice-daily runs along the water's edge. I now often fell asleep before eleven p.m. most evenings. It was a little cooler than the last time I'd been there, since summer was drawing to an end. Nothing had changed my love for the gorgeous views, which I continued to admire daily, not quite believing that they were going to be a permanent fixture in my life.

Now that I was alone, I could freely admit that I searched for possible sightings of Morgan whenever I was on the beach. Since the summer season was coming to a close, there weren't many people around. I hadn't had the time, or the courage, to head into town to go to the bookshop, and I had no one to go clubbing with, so I spent my time alone with the dogs, getting the house in order.

I'd not found a job that interested me yet, but I wasn't lounging around doing nothing with my spare time. After deciding where all my stuff needed to go, I began to move around the furniture that came with the house, changing the rooms to suit me. I noticed that most of the furnishings weren't in the greatest condition and would need replacing soon, but there were some pieces that, with a bit of hard work and a lot of T.L.C., could be refurbished and modernised. While I worked on the dining chairs, I discovered that I not only enjoyed the work; I was quite good at it, too — well, for a beginner.

May, the previous owner, dropped by the house with some papers she'd forgotten to give me when I'd collected the keys from her. She saw the chairs on the porch slathered in paint remover and the bright red material hanging over the balustrade, and she began to coo over my efforts. I blushed and told her it was just a hobby to keep me busy until I found a job. Ignoring me, she gushed at how much nicer everything was going to look. She then informed me that she was going to see if there was anything in her house that needed "sprucing up," and she'd bring it over once I'd finished with my own furniture.

I'd been in the house for just over a month when the boiler gave up with a few clunks, which were followed by a bang loud enough to scare the dogs.

Swearing like a sailor, I pulled an oversized sweater over my running gear before rummaging around for a phone directory. Forty-five minutes later, I gave up and called May to ask for the number for a plumber. She promised to send over "her usual guy" to take a look, but it wasn't until I'd ended the call that I realised who that guy would be.

Sure enough, Morgan clambered out of the van that pulled into my drive as soon as the engine cut off. I could feel my hands getting clammy while I watched him walk to the back of the van and drag out a tool box before he slammed and locked the doors. A lump formed in my throat when he walked up the stairs to knock on the front door.

The moment his knuckles made contact with the freshly painted door, the house erupted in ear-shattering barks, and the dogs fought amongst themselves to reach the door first. I waded my way through and pulled it open.

"Is it safe to come in?" he asked with a grin.

"Of course it is. Their bark's worse than their bite." I whistled for the dogs' attention and commanded them to sit before standing to one side, manoeuvring myself so Morgan could enter. I couldn't help but smile when he hesitated.

"So, they *do* bite?" He eyed the dogs with a nervous look on his face, but they wandered into the kitchen for a drink.

"They don't; I promise."

Morgan looked around when he walked into the hallway, obviously checking out the changes I'd made since moving in.

"It looks good."

"You sound almost shocked," I teased.

"Oh, no. There's no way I'm ever going to share any of my preconceived notions with you ever again. I value my life!"

I burst out laughing at the look of mock fear on his face, and we made our way upstairs to the boiler. I couldn't help but admire him while I followed him up the steps, and I shivered when I remembered how he'd looked the last time I had seen him: tanned, topless, and more than a little bit drunk.

જી૦ન્ટ

"What made you move down here? Most people from round here want to move to London," Morgan said when we sat on the back porch, fresh cups of coffee clutched between our hands. The hazel eyes that had been haunting me were now casting wary glances toward the dogs, who were snuffling around the small area I had fenced off at the back of the house.

"I don't think there's just one reason. I felt so comfortable here in the summer. Having the time and space to myself allowed me to realise how many changes I needed to make in my life. As hard as that was, I think that was the start."

"Are you happy now?" He caught my frown and mistook it for anger at his question. "Sorry, I didn't mean to ask that."

"It's fine." I waved my hand, dismissing his unnecessary apology. "I was just a little surprised by you adding 'now' to your question." I turned my body so that I was facing him.

"There was always something about you when you were here in the summer, even when you were having fun. It was almost like you were holding back from having fun, which isn't something I'm used to seeing."

His words left me a little unnerved. I hadn't expected him to be able to read me so well and in such a short space of time.

"I had a lot on my mind back then, but working through my problems and deciding to move here helped more than I'd expected. All I need now is to find myself a half-decent job." I watched the dogs playing, worried I'd blurted out too much.

"As long as you're happy and settled, now you're here."

"I'm getting there." I whistled for the dogs when I felt the rain start. Morgan seemed to sense that I'd had enough of a heart-to-heart and gathered his stuff. I walked through the house with the dogs and watched while Morgan drove away, grateful he appeared to understand me.

It took a total of four visits from Morgan over a two-week period to order all the correct parts and completely fix the boiler. The first three visits were followed by tea or coffee and a long, relaxing chat on the porch. Not once did it feel weird to spend time with him that way, and he never complained about having to come over after being stuck at the bookshop all day. Before his final visit, I decided to cook him a light dinner, as my way of saying thanks for both his hard work and company.

# Chapter 13

# Act Four, Scene Three

I cooked up a simple meal to thank Morgan for the help and the talks. The thank-you meal I made was only a curry, but I hoped Morgan would see how grateful I was for all the time he'd spent with his head in my airing cupboard, making sure the boiler was properly fixed.

Leaving the food to simmer on low heat, I went out onto the porch to continue spray painting some picture frames I'd found in the loft that May no longer wanted. I knew I wouldn't have long to paint now that it was getting dark earlier, so I made fast work of it. When I finished, there was still just enough light for me clean up the mess I'd made.

I left the frames propped up against the banister to dry and ran into the kitchen to grab a rubbish bag. Just as I began picking up the newspaper I'd used to protect the porch from the silver spray paint, Morgan's van pulled up three feet away from me, bathing me in the light from his headlamps.

"Hi. Sorry I'm late. The bookshop ended up a bit trashed today."

I watched him unfold himself from the driver's seat. He stretched just enough to flash a strip of skin above the waistband of his jeans.

"Hey. It's fine. Thanks for coming over after work." I hesitated mentioning the meal I'd prepared for him, feeling nervous for some reason.

"Right; I'm gonna head up to get this boiler sorted before it gets too dark to even see it."

I let him past me, and then continued picking up my rubbish. Once I'd dumped the bag at the side of the house, I went in to check on the rice. Everything was looking perfect, and I could feel my stomach turning over in anticipation when Morgan entered.

"That was quick," I commented, stirring the curry.

"I just needed to reset the thermostat. It should last for years now."

I could feel his eyes on me while I moved around the kitchen, making a drink.

"Something smells good."

"There's plenty, if you're hungry." There was no way I was going to admit I'd cooked a special meal for him. I handed him a fresh coffee, unable to make eye contact.

"That would be fantastic. I haven't eaten since lunchtime."

I gestured for him to take a seat before I dished up. This was a bit different from the chats we'd had sitting on the step of my porch over coffee. It felt more . . . *intimate,* even though, on the surface, it wasn't.

"This looks great. I can never be bothered to cook, so I tend to live on sandwiches and cereal." Morgan flashed a wide, bright grin at me before diving into the food on his plate.

I couldn't help but chuckle to myself when the dogs slinked in and sat at Morgan's feet, gazing up at him in the hope he'd drop a piece of chicken or two.

∽⤫

"Oh, shit!" Morgan suddenly jumped up from the sofa where we had both been seated, sipping bottles of beer after dinner. "It's almost midnight."

I glanced up at the clock above the stereo, which was playing low music in the background. We'd been talking for over three hours. When I stood, the movement disturbed the dogs, who began whinging to go outside. Shoving on my shoes, I prepared to take them for a quick walk out on the beach.

"How did that happen?" I asked, smiling while I watched him grab his tools and jacket.

"I blame you, the fantastic food, and beer. Oh, crap. I can't drive." We'd both had at least three bottles of beer; that, coupled with the darkness, was a no-no for driving.

"Let me just get the dogs out, then I'll call you a cab."

"Thanks, Ava." Morgan collapsed back onto the sofa. I led the dogs to the back door and let them outside. I'd only been standing watching them for five minutes when I turned back to see that Morgan had fallen asleep. Whistling for the dogs to come back in, I then grabbed a blanket to cover Morgan and headed up to bed.

The following morning, I woke to a silent house. I was used to the dogs whining to be let outside as soon as I even considered opening my eyes. Not this morning. It was a little unnerving. I sat up to discover it was almost ten. In a blind panic, I threw the duvet off and rushed downstairs, only to find all three dogs curled up in bed, fast asleep. Confused, I grabbed the kettle, filled it, and put it on to boil. A note had been stuck to my favourite mug.

*Ava, thanks for the sofa and the blanket. I took the dogs for a walk to let you have a lie-in. Catch you soon. M*

Not knowing quite how to react, I sat on the porch with my steaming mug of tea, rereading Morgan's note. I was touched that he'd thought of the dog's needs, but I was confused about why he didn't leave them to wake me up as usual. I wouldn't have minded; I was more than used to it.

It wasn't until I mentioned it to Erica over the phone later that day that I considered the possibility that there was something more behind it.

"He's trying to let you know that he wants you to be happy . . . More than as a friend." Erica's voice sounded like there was a strong possibility that she was doing a happy dance while she spoke.

"I think he was just being kind."

"You keep telling yourself that, Ava. I think, and always have thought, that Morgan quite fancies you."

"Oh, my God. Are you twelve?" I rolled my eyes at her choice of words before realising she couldn't see me.

"Shut your face. Look, he's gorgeous — sorry Liam — so why don't you give it a go?"

"Erica, stop playing matchmaker. I have to go; I need my run. I'll call you later," I said, ending the call with a white lie. I didn't need a run, but I did need to get away from Erica's meddling. Ever since I'd decided to move to the beach house, she'd blathered on about me and Morgan getting together. She was like a sixteen-year-old finding out her friend was going on a first date.

I decided to head out for a walk to try and clear my head of Morgan's note and Erica's words. Leaving the dogs in the house, I set off along the beach, wearing my headphones as usual. Quickly losing myself in the cold wind and the music playing in my ears, I looked out across the ocean but didn't see really anything. I tried not to think about how attracted to Morgan I was, or about how much that attraction grew every time I saw him. The more we spoke and got to know each other, the more I wanted him to kiss me.

After an hour or so of walking, I came to a halt and just watched the water. I'd never felt so peaceful than right at that moment, even with everything that had been going through my mind. No matter what happened, I knew for a fact that I wasn't going to ever regret moving to the beach. I closed my eyes and took a few deep breaths. Although I wasn't into meditation, I could see the appeal sometimes.

Someone tapped me on the shoulder, and I jumped almost three feet into the air. I turned to see Morgan standing behind me, smiling. Pulling off my headphones, I prepared to give him a mouthful of abuse for scaring me, but before I managed to get a word out, he grabbed my face with gentle hands and kissed me.

# Epilogue

## Closing Credits

Eighteen months later . . .

I straightened my hair and blotted my lipstick before slipping on my sandals. My stomach was flipping from nerves, but I managed to ignore it while I added the finishing touches.

Erica walked into the room. "You look gorgeous," she gushed, handing me my posy of flowers. "You better not be trying to upstage me."

I watched while she fussed with her beautifully simple dress. It was made from ivory satin, floor length and just breathtaking. She made a beautiful bride, and this time I knew it was going to be forever. Liam was the complete opposite of Michael. He treated Erica like a princess, yet he didn't put up with her stroppy side. Michael had let her get away with anything so that he could have a quiet life and sleep around, Liam often called her on her snippiness.

I was over the moon for her and honoured that she wanted to have the wedding at the beach house. It was just their families, close friends, and the priest. Erica had the big ceremony and honeymoon the first time round; all she wanted and needed this time was Liam.

"Like I could upstage you. You are the picture-perfect blushing bride." I wrapped my arms around her and pulled her into a tight hug.

"Oh, I think you could." She held my shoulders at arm's length and looked down. My distended stomach was wedged in between us, prominently displayed by the cut of my powder-blue dress.

"No one will look twice at me — I'm fat. You're gorgeous." I reached a hand up to fix a loose strand of hair.

"I can think of one person who will. More than twice."

I couldn't help but smile at the thought of Morgan. No one even needed to mention his name to get a reaction from me. After spending the last year and a half being wooed and courted — even after we were a "real" couple — he still surprised me with picnics on the beach and stuck little notes in my lunch bag while I got ready for another day at the shop I'd opened a few months previous.

After that first kiss on the beach, we'd taken each day as it came without even talking about it. We fell into a natural routine, simply slotting each other into our lives. It had hit me that being with Morgan meant that every inhabitant of the small town I now called home knew everything about me and our new life together. The locals would stop me in the street, smile at me, and then ask me to pass on a message to him about lining up a new handyman job. Each and every person who popped by the house or my shop would tell me how happy they were to see Morgan settled down.

When we found out I was pregnant, it seemed to affect everyone. I'd never been given so many gifts and cards before; one old dear even made us a cake to congratulate us. It was bizarre, but I couldn't imagine my life being any different.

"Are you ready?" I asked Erica when our preparation time was almost up.

"I've been ready for over two years. Let's get this show on the road, and then we can party." Erica laughed at the face I pulled, knowing that I wouldn't be doing any partying after the wedding. "I'm sorry, honey."

"Don't be. Just be happy."

The ceremony on the sand went off without a problem. Once the photographs had been taken, I led everyone back to the house, where I had laid on a simple buffet. Morgan had managed to hook up his sound system to a set of huge speakers so that the party could continue on into the evening. I chatted to the guests, making sure their food and drinks were regularly topped up and that everyone was having a good time. Erica didn't need to worry about being a hostess; I wanted her to be able to just revel in being centre of attention.

When the music for the first dance began, I stood on the porch, looking out at the guests while the sun began to set. The whole picture before me looked like a scene from a movie. I jumped a little when Morgan's strong arms wrapped around my expanding waist and drew me back against his hard chest. No words were spoken while we watched our friends enjoy the evening.

Sometimes life takes a new direction out of nowhere, just like in the movies.

*The End*
*Exit, Stage Left*

# Haunted Raine

## By R.E. Hargrave

# Acknowledgements:

This novella is dedicated to my father
Smallwood Graham Carroll III.
You always told me I could be anything I
wanted – even a starship captain – and
together we forged a love of South Carolina
ghost stories which are memories I hold dear.
Combining my dreams and my memories led to
*Haunted Raine.*
I think of you often, and miss you always. RIP
1945 – 1987

~*~*~*~

This tale would not have seen the light of a day
if not for several key people:
My family: Michael, Nathaniel, Nicholas, and
Meredith I love you with all of my heart.
Thanks for being patient with my crazy
schedule!
JC Clarke: The cover is breathtaking, and I
can't imagine taking this journey without you
by my side. Pinky Swear!
Massy Reyes: Your knowledge and input were a
salve to my sanity!
Renaissance Romance Publishing: For editing,
guidance, support, and just all around taking a
chance on me.
Thank you, all!

# *Prologue*

They were supposed to be our Golden Years, but I didn't feel so golden. Perhaps "weathered" would be a better description. At fifty-two years old, I could admit that I wasn't in the same condition I'd been in when beginning this life with Richard thirty-one years earlier—that was for sure.

Richard Morrissey—Rick to his close friends and family—wore his fifty-seven years quite well. He still stood just over six feet—the aging slump had not yet taken a hold of him—and he was taller than me by three inches if I wasn't slouching.

His hair had gone silver in a distinguished manner. The color looked good, peppered through his natural brown hair, sexy even, and somehow made his blue eyes pop. Rick's fastidious nature demanded structure and order in his life, and pushed him to continue using the gym with regularity. It showed in the strong lines of his back and chest.

With my high forehead, wide nose, and brown eyes, I had no delusions as to which one of us was the better looking. At least I'd always been able to keep a nice tan. If I so much as thought about stepping out into the sun a golden glow appeared and if I spent any real time outside, I'd become a deep bronze. My body was softer around the edges than Rick's, the 'girls' swung lower, and my hair was a bland gray—or it would've been if it weren't for my good friend Clairol and her honey-blonde magic in a bottle. Once a month, I went down to the beauty school with my pharmacy bag in hand and had my roots done for a fraction of what it would cost me to support the snooty salon across town.

Yes, I had an issue with frugality. I'd learned how to get by on very little in our humble beginnings. While Richard went to law school, I picked up odd jobs here and there, taking what I could get with an infant in tow. In due time, Richard passed the Bar Exam with flying colors, but we continued to just get by while he started off as a legal clerk and then worked his way up to partner over the years.

Even when we found we had more money than we knew what to do with, I continued to clip coupons and eagle-eye the sale racks. I'd done it for too many years not to anymore. The upside to my penny-pinching was that when we wanted, or needed something, we had the funds. Extra-curricular school activities, cars, and putting three kids through college were never a cause of stress for us.

Extended summer vacations became our one big splurge each year. Rick would take all of his annual vacation time when the kids were out for summer break, and we would travel the world for two months. Richard Junior—Ricky—got his first passport when he was ten, Lucas and Lily had been seven, and we'd taken them all to Australia.

By the time the kids left for college, their passports were full of stamps, and the photo albums overflowed. We'd had an abundance of experiences and had made enough memories to last a lifetime. This was turning out to be a good thing, because the last few years . . .

Well, things had become strained between Rick and I—almost like we'd forgotten how we'd been in our younger days, and now needed the kids with us for any sense of togetherness. So many years of our lives had been spent as a family unit of five that somehow Rick and I had let 'us' fade away.

The kids had been out of the house for a good five years by now. Lily, being the last one to leave, had stayed at home and gone to Converse College for her first degree. Our boys had both left straight away from high school. Ricky had received a full ride to Rice in Texas, and Lucas had joined the Marine Corps, which had taken him to Parris Island in South Carolina for recruit training.

Rick worked a lot. In fact, it had been about eight years since we'd done one of our summer long vacations. His leave had hit a point of rolling as much over as could be, and then losing the rest. He had about three months saved up and sitting on the books.

My days were now spent quilting and volunteering over at Spartanburg Regional as a candy-striper twice a week, instead of running the PTA and chaperoning school field trips. I also spent a fair amount of time at the library.

Family roots—and the history that went

with them—fascinated me because of my great-grandmother Nancy Shaw. She'd been abandoned as a newborn by the front doors of a hospital in Charleston, South Carolina, so I knew nothing of my own roots further back than that.

It was always an adventure to study different lineages and pretend that perhaps I was learning my own. The Gullah culture in the Carolina low-country was my current obsession. Hailing from Africa, Haiti, and the Dominican Republic, the people who could now be found in areas of New York—such as Harlem, Queens, and Brooklyn—seemed at some point to end up down in South Carolina and Georgia. One thing I knew for sure: their history was rich with intrigue, scandal, and religion—Voodoo in particular.

Of course, there was more than just the library as a source of information available to me. The older patients at the hospital were a veritable fountain of knowledge. Which is why, at the suggestion of a patient I was visiting with one day, I came home with a proposition for my husband—and our wayward marriage—that would also further the pursuit of knowledge in my current subject matter. To be honest, I was surprised when Rick agreed. However, two months later, when the peak tourist season wound down at the end of July, we found ourselves the proud owners of a one-bedroom beach bungalow. It was on the coast of South Carolina, in the small town of St. Helena, a thriving Gullah community.

The catch to the low price we got the property for being that it was a fixer-upper. We'd bought it for dirt cheap, and the plan was to spend the next three months refurbishing it, with the intent to put it up for sale. If the flip went well, we thought perhaps this could become our new annual 'thing' with the added bonus that it would serve to be a good investment heading into our retirement years.

If we'd only known what was in store for us and how our lives would be turned upside down because of it.

# Chapter 1

# Welcome to St. Helena

The central part of St. Helena had been developed with tourists in mind. Novelty shops, bars, and tattoo parlors all lined the seawall road. Our new house sat about five miles north of town on a private stretch of beach front.

Most of the two acre property was overrun with large cypress trees, whose branches slumped under the heavy weight of Spanish moss. In the waning afternoon sunlight, the shadows created by the vegetation made it easy to imagine a wispy figure shrouded in the moss, watching me while I walked from the car to the house.

I paused and squinted while fumbling for the glasses perched in my hair. By the time my specs were on my face, the image was gone, and I laughed at the cold shiver that caught me off guard. The air was the typical muggy warmth found on the coastline this time of year, and I was sure the chills had come from the fact that we'd just spent several hours in our air-conditioned Lexus RX 450h.

Just because we were secure financially didn't mean we couldn't do our part for the environment by purchasing hybrid cars. Rick had left his sportier ES 300h at home.

With a shrug, I moved to the porch and dug out the key the realtor had sent us with our closing paperwork, unlocked the door — with some effort since it was sticking — and entered. Goosebumps broke out on my arms, and the dull throb of a lurking headache pulsed in time with my heartbeat.

*It'll be an adventure. We'll have fun.*

I had to remind myself of the words I'd used to beg Rick to give this crazy idea of mine a try while I looked around the dusty and dank living room.

"Lorraine, how much should I . . ." Rick's voice halted behind me as he took his first look at the place.

I turned with an apologetic expression in place. "We knew it needed work when we bought it so cheap."

Nothing was said for a few minutes while we looked at each other from two feet apart.

"Raine . . ."

I didn't like the emotion in his eyes: tired and doubtful.

"We've got a busy three months ahead," I offered with a slight smile and a shrug, trying to sound upbeat.

He sighed and nodded in a show of reluctant defeat.

I hadn't asked him to go on a murdering spree — just to spend some time with me without dockets, depositions, case files, and everything else that had become the center of his world. Stubborn as ever, I plodded forward, ignoring the vibe coming off him, which made it clear he didn't want to be there right now.

"Let's do a quick walk through and get a starter list together. We'll make a run to the store so we can get settled in tonight, and then have an early start in the morning. I noticed a Wal-Mart on the way here through town. It's off the main drag."

"Sure, Raine. Whatever. I'll just get the rest of the luggage brought in while you start on your list." With that, he set down the two cases he'd carried in and disappeared back through the rickety door, the screen door emitting an abrasive squeak as it resisted use.

"Rick," I called after him, but he didn't stop.

I reached over to try the light switch next to the door and half expected the room to stay shrouded in darkness. A single, exposed light bulb, which was screwed into a ceiling plate over the area to the right — I assumed it was the dining room — lit up with a dull glow. The chain that hung next to it made me think of a scene out of a horror movie.

Moving under the dim light, I opened my purse to locate my pen and notepad, and my hands bumped the hidden box of Marlboros at the bottom. I looked at them with longing, but knew Rick would be back inside any minute so I'd have to wait.

If Rick knew I'd taken up smoking about a year ago, I'd be in for a lecture for sure. Of course, the fact that I *had* been smoking for a year and he hadn't caught on spoke volumes.

*Can't smell it on someone if you never get*

*close to them, though.*

Ignoring the smokes for the time-being, I grabbed my supplies and dropped my purse in the corner of the room. Deciding my present position was the best place to start, I surveyed the area, and then began.

In no time, I'd paced the room from one side to the other while counting off my heel-to-toe steps to get an estimated thirty feet across and twenty feet wide. The front door was centered on the wide space. There were two windows, one each in the dining room and the living room, covered with aluminum foil. No other light fixtures adorned the front area, and apart from the luggage, there was nothing in the space except for a metal folding chair discarded in the far corner.

Right. Putting pen to paper, I wrote down assorted cleaning supplies: broom, mop, extra-large Pine Sol, trash bags, sponges, and cloths. For preliminary aesthetics, I added a floor lamp, curtain rods, and sheers. I was hoping to find a local thrift store to pick up some basic furnishings when we were ready for them.

It was hard to see the condition of the walls in the bad lighting, but I was pretty sure paint was a given and added the supplies to the list. If I was lucky, I might be able to get Rick to start painting while I went on that furniture hunt.

Next, I went into the kitchen, also lit with an exposed, single low-watt bulb. Something scurried away when the light flared to life and the screen door slammed, making me jump.

"I'm in the kitchen," I called out, and wasn't surprised when I got no answer. The man was hard-pressed to speak anymore, unless it was business related.

Upon attempting to open the refrigerator door, it stuck, taking a forceful yank to get it to pop open. A moldy smell hit my nose and I gagged. Mouse droppings littered the counter tops and dead bugs filled the stove grates.

New appliances were going to be a requirement. They didn't have to be top of the line, but there was no way we'd resell the place with those. I scrawled 'Kitchen — full overhaul' on my notepad, and headed across the short hallway to the bathroom.

It wasn't in much better shape than the kitchen. The toilet was discolored and had no water in it; the small, mirrored medicine cabinet was splotchy and cracked from the silver on the back being damaged. Looking down to the floor, the linoleum was yellowed and curling up from the edges, and had several small burn marks.

I might have fallen in love when I spotted the tub. It would be staying. A classic claw-foot, it was nice and deep with a circular frame at the top for a curtain to be attached. By some miracle, it was even clean for the most part when I looked inside. Pleased with the discovery and having added my notes for the bathroom to my list, I started to turn and go check the bedroom when movement outside the window caught my eye.

Uncovered, the window started about three

feet up from the top edge of the tub and overlooked a view filled with more of the mossy cypress trees. Even with my glasses, the fading light made it near impossible to see outside so I stepped into the tub to get closer.

A gurgling sound rumbled in the pipes and I spun around, slipping and falling in the tub just as yellowish-brown water started pouring from the faucet. I landed on my ample rear and moved to scramble backward, standing back up before my pants got wet. After climbing out of the tub, I turned the handle, and the water shut off.

*That's weird. It's like someone turned it on.*

The front door slammed again. "Lorraine, we're losing light and I'm hungry!"

With a last glance out the window, I turned off the light, and then hurried to the front. There was no hiding a noticeable limp. My left hip hurt. I was going to be bruised.

"What happened to you?"

"Oh, I slipped on something. No big deal, let's just go," I answered, avoiding telling him the truth. It wouldn't be too farfetched for him to declare the tub a safety hazard and want to get rid of it.

When I went to get my purse, I stopped short. It wasn't where I'd left it. "Rick, did you move my purse?"

"Huh? Why would I do that?" he grouched.

I had to turn in a full circle before I noticed it on the folding chair. Shaking my head at my forgetfulness, I grabbed my purse, and we left in search of Wal-Mart and food.

# Chapter 2

# Funny Feelings

The next morning, I awoke stiff from sleeping on the floor after the air had seeped out of the mattress during the night. It was still dark; the sun not having made an appearance yet. Rick seemed unfazed by the less than favorable sleeping conditions and snored away in his spot. I chalked it up to his love of camping. Men just seemed better with that kind of thing.

After making my way to the bathroom, I relieved myself — thankful I'd had Rick add water to the tank the night before — and did the best I could, with a damp paper towel, to wipe-down my body. Until we had a plumber out to look at the pipes, I wasn't going to attempt a shower, let alone a bath. Besides, I'd forgotten to grab some cheap towels, and we'd agreed to start with the bathroom and kitchen since they shared a common wall of plumbing. Both rooms pretty much needed to be gutted, so today was going to be grimy work.

Wincing at the movement of my jeans sliding over my hips, I looked down to see that I'd called it on the bruise. My hip was a kaleidoscope of burgeoning colors. *Awesome.*

The view out of the window was blurred by the haziness of a pre-sunrise fog that I knew would burn off as the day warmed up. Despite the limited visibility, I still found my gaze being drawn to a clump of trees and a structure off to the left. There had been no mention of any outbuildings when we'd bought the property. I became dizzy, and for the briefest moment, thought I heard whispering.

Curious, I hurried back to the bedroom to get my shoes on, and then made my way outside, grabbing my purse as an afterthought while I rushed out the front door. Plotting a course toward the back of the lot, my feet carried me forward as my hand dipped into my purse to find my smokes. I came back empty-handed.

Coming to a standstill, I dug deeper in my purse, but to no avail. Just as I began to worry that either Rick had found them or they'd somehow fallen out when we were out the night before, a loon cried out in the distance and my head snapped up. Through the haze, I could just make out a worn, yellow shack.

With the cigarettes forgotten, I resumed walking, but the shack never got closer. By the time I reached the area where I could've sworn I'd seen it, I was standing in front of a charred foundation. A breeze picked up and the ends of my short blonde ponytail blew across my neck. Wrapping my arms around my middle, I shivered, and then gasped when my eyes landed on a red box poking up from between some bricks.

With a shaky hand, I leaned over and tugged on it. Marlboros. At the sound of a cackling laugh, I turned and ran back toward the house and the car. There had to be an explanation. Something along the lines of prankster teenagers were using the spot to sneak smokes, and the laugh, well, it was a bird or some other wildlife. My mind was just conjuring craziness because I hadn't slept well, it was early, and I needed coffee. Lots of coffee.

Hitting the edge of the house, I chanced a glance back over my shoulder and could make out the faint yellowed edges of the shack once again. This time, a dark-skinned figure shrouded in white, stood off to the side of it. Pain pierced my head.

Once, twice, I blinked, and the shack and the mysterious figure were gone.

*Something's not quite right here,* was the thought in my head while I slipped into the car and prepared to go hunt down some coffee and breakfast.

Ten minutes later, I was coming to the end of the long drive. The road was composed of tight-packed sand and lined with majestic trees whose branches stretched overhead creating a living canopy. Braking, I looked to the right to check for traffic, and saw the red box in the passenger's seat next to my bag.

I couldn't remember keeping it in my hands as I ran, or driving for that matter. My nerves were shot, so I pulled over to the side of the road. Desperate for the anxiety-calming nicotine, my hands wouldn't stop shaking as I worked a cigarette free of the box and tucked it between my lips. At the same time, I smashed the car lighter in, willing it to heat.

Thirty seconds elapsed before it popped up and I concentrated on getting my smoke lit, then inhaled with deep gratitude. The first one disappeared in a rapid series of puff and inhale. My hands settled, I lit a second cigarette, and then pulled out onto the road headed for town. There had to be a drive through somewhere that I could grab Rick and me a coffee and some food.

When I saw the sign for Momma Faye's Café, I pulled in, more than happy to skip on the triple-bypass fare offered at the fast food chains. By the time the bell on the door dinged the announcement of my entry, the scents of bacon and strong coffee were putting my frazzled nerves to rest.

"Mornin', Miss. Just one?"

The bright grin and big, curious brown eyes of the dreadlocked boy — he couldn't have been more than fifteen, sixteen at the most — couldn't be ignored, and I returned it.

"Yes, thank you."

He grabbed a menu, a pre-rolled silverware packet, and led me to a table. "This okay?"

I nodded and slid into one of the chairs, my smile holding as a waitress came up with a pot of coffee and flipped the mug over on my table to fill it.

The boy handed me the menu, mumbling "Enjoy," and scurried off, leaving me with the waitress, whose nametag indicated she was

Dixie.

She looked like a Dixie with her cut-off shorts and over-sized plaid button-up shirt which knotted at her waist. Her lips moved while she chomped on a piece of a gum and laid out the blue-plate specials for the day.

Knowing I shouldn't, but unable to resist, I ordered myself a plate of their peach stuffed French toast with a side of extra bacon. Oh, and a chocolate milk to wash it down with. Thinking Rick might enjoy some local fare instead of one of his soy-protein and wheat germ shake things he always had, I pre-ordered him an Island omelet plate to go. With shrimp, caramelized onions, and brie cheese how could he not be happy with my choice? It also came with a side of course ground grits and some fried green tomatoes.

I was hopeful that getting Rick to submerse himself in the local way of life would be beneficial in getting him to unwind so that we could both enjoy this vacation. My thoughts turned to what would be the best way to approach the things we needed to get done today, and soon enough the food arrived. Digging in, one thing crossed my mind: *Holy shit was this stuff good!*

At that point, I think I wandered off into a food coma because all train of thought stopped. It was all about the flavor in my mouth and nothing else. Until Big Grin plopped into the seat across from me, that was.

"You buy the old Hughes place?"

Taken aback by his abrupt appearance, I

swallowed the bite of bacon in my mouth, and then wiped the corners with my napkin. "I'm sorry, you are?"

"Sorry, Ma'am. Name's Samuel Fontaine. This here's my momma's place," he added the last bit with evident pride. "It's just that the Hughes place's been up fer grabs for a long spell now, and with you's bein' not from round 'ere . . ." Samuel trailed off, looking down in his lap.

"Well, I don't know if the house we purchased belonged to the Hughes family, but yes, we just acquired a one-bedroom house about five miles north of town."

Samuel's head snapped up, excitement clear in his eyes. "That's it. Have ya seen anythin'?" His voice was just above a whisper.

My appetite vanished at the innocent question.

# Chapter 3

## Peach Pie

The re-pumped air mattress felt like a cloud under my back, and I groaned without remorse while I stretched my toes toward the wall and elongated my spine.

"Thought you hated that thing?" Rick said with a light, teasing tone.

"Yeah, well, after the day we've had, rocks would probably feel good so long as I could lay out straight on them."

Rick chuckled and shook his head at me. "But doesn't it feel good to know so much was accomplished today, Raine?"

I nodded while my eyes followed the movement of Rick's hands divesting himself of first his dirty, smudged up tee, and then his jeans. He left his underpants on and strutted from the room. The telltale straining of the pipes let me know he'd crossed the hall to the bathroom.

While I waited for Rick to come to bed, I thought back over the day, and all that had transpired since meeting Samuel. It had taken me several moments to get the lump out of my throat when he'd dropped that bomb of a question on me, but once I had, I'd reacted pretty quickly.

*"Whatever do you mean, Samuel?"* I hedged while taking a sip of my chocolate milk.

*"Ya know, ma'am, things . . ."* His eyes widened at me, suggesting, with heavy emphasis, that we weren't talking about normal, everyday things.

*"Sure —"* Samuel wanted to be evasive, so could I. *"There are lots of trees covered in what looks like dried out gray strings —"*

*"That'd be the moss,"* he cut me off, and I rolled my eyes. *"I was talkin' about weird things."*

*"Samuel, how much are you making here?"* I changed tactics.

*"Whatchu mean?"*

*"Pay, Samuel. What are you getting paid to be the host?"*

He smiled and his teeth caught my attention again. The kid had great dental health. *"Oh, nuthin'. Momma lets me hang out and help when I want. Sometimes I can get a slice o' her peach pie fer my efforts."*

Perfect.

*"Would you like to make some money?"* His look was quizzical so I kept going. *"My name is Lorraine Morrissey. My husband Rick and I are flipping that house we just bought. We could use a strong, young back; not to mention, I imagine you know your way around and could point us in the right direction for good deals on supplies?"*

*I took another bite of my sinful toast while he thought about my offer. I almost choked when he replied, with utmost sincerity, "Will I get pie, Missus Lorraine?"*

Half an hour later, I'd met Faye Fontaine, founder and proprietor of Momma Faye's, and Samuel was in my car with a whole peach pie in his lap. Rick's breakfast was packed up in the backseat. Faye had been generous and thrown in a large thermos of coffee and a gallon of sweet tea, too.

Faye and I had hit it off in an instant, and I'd found it easy to talk with her like we were old friends. Chatting with Faye had started filling in some of the blanks, and I was hoping to learn more while Samuel helped Rick and me out in the upcoming days.

Rick came back from the bathroom with a confused look furrowing his brow.

"Everything okay, babe?"

His neck swiveled to look back out in the hall, but he didn't answer me right away.

"Richard?"

"Uh? Oh, yeah. Sorry, Raine, just . . . never mind. Like you said, it's been a long day and my muscles are twitching from all the extra use."

"Did you see something?" I asked as the goose bumps erupted up and down my arms.

My question must have been spot on because his eyes snapped to mine. "Yeah, I think. I don't know. I was brushing my teeth and thought I heard a tapping on the window. When I looked up, I could've sworn I saw a face peeking in, but I blinked and it was gone." A half laugh tumbled from his lips. "I'm sure it was —"

"Nothing. I mean, I'm sure it wasn't anything. Just being in unfamiliar surroundings is messing with our heads." The words blurted out of my mouth, cutting him off. "Come to bed." I pulled back the blankets on his side of the mattress and patted the exposed space.

Rick crawled in next to me, stretching much as I had done, and even letting out a similar relieved moan. The sound made long neglected things tickle deep inside me. "Gotta say, it was a stroke of luck you running into Samuel. He saved us days' worth of work with all he did today."

*Was Rick complimenting me on a decision I'd made?*

"He seemed like a good kid. Real knowledgeable, too." I added the last part, still unsure if I wanted to fess up to the strange occurrences from last night and this morning. Seeing as Rick had his own instance of weirdness now, I was inclined, maybe. "Doesn't hurt that his mom is an amazing cook, either."

With a smile, Rick turned to me and pulled me into his arms. The unfamiliar affection was alarming, and I tensed, causing him to sigh and begin to loosen his arms.

"No. Please don't pull away. You just . . . I wasn't ready for that."

For a moment, his blue eyes became cloudy and looked hurt in the pale moonlight. "What happened to us, Raine?"

I swallowed, and the gulp was audible in the quiet space between us. We needed to have this talk, but was now the time? *Would there be a better time?*

"Time and children," I shrugged, "distance."

"Lorraine, angel face . . ." He stared down at me with a sad smile while using the old endearment.

I closed my eyes at the warm feeling that coursed through me.

"This is all my fault, isn't it?" Rick whispered.

"Oh, Rick. No. I'm just as much at fault —" Rick's lips crashing against mine, pressing them in against my teeth with a breath stealing roughness, cut off my protest. I sighed into the kiss, reveling in the heat crackling along my arms as my nerve endings zinged with sensation.

His hand had just started to inch up under the hem of my top, fingers grazing the inward curve of my waist, when there was a loud boom outside. Our ragged breaths picked up speed as we broke our kiss and stared at each other.

"Rick, what was that?" I pushed my husband's hand away from where it rested on my hip, and rolled off the mattress onto my knees. My lower back muscles screamed in retaliation as my thigh muscles didn't want to cooperate in getting me upright.

"Not su —" His answer was stilted by a crackling, hissing sound seconds before the bedroom window filled with a blazing orange light.

Time seemed to freeze while our attentions locked on the scene outside, waiting for comprehension to dawn. When it did for me, I went into fight or flight mode. "Oh, shit. Fire! Come on, Rick, we've got to get out of here!" I yelled from my spot on the floor while cursing my aging bones.

Fit and agile, he had no problems leaping to his feet. Maybe there was something to his exercise and healthy eating. If we made it through tonight, I would start changing my ways. The thought was random, but my mind was trying to focus on anything but the vibrant orange and yellow inferno that had come out of nowhere.

"Up you go," Rick whispered in my ear while his hands scooped under my arms and yanked me up. Once I was steady on my feet, he grabbed my hand and we hurried out to the front rooms, ripping the front door open before rushing outside.

A large fire blazed about twenty feet away from the bathroom window, where we'd stacked the trash and other demolition debris from the day. I turned to go back inside for my cell phone to call 911, but slipped on something on the ground. Rick's quick reflexes kept me from crashing to my knees, and we both looked down at the same time.

A squashed box of Marlboros and a toss away lighter were displayed on the ground in mocking accusation.

"What the . . ?" Rick trailed off, his eyes

searching the dark areas to either side of the flames. "Hello! Who's out there? Show yourselves!" he yelled into the night. A bright zigzag ripped across the dark sky, illuminating everything for about five seconds.

My gut instinct told me there was nobody out there, no one who would answer anyways.

# Chapter 4

## Reconnecting

Two a.m. found Rick and I beyond exhausted. I'd thought we were tired the first time we tried to go to bed, but after another five hours of police and firemen, nosy neighbors, and managing to get a room at the local Motel 6 because I refused to stay at the house until things were sorted out; I couldn't get in bed fast enough.

Not even the lure of running pipes and hot water stopped the two of us from falling on top of the floral print comforters and passing out the moment the door lock clicked behind us.

✂❦

Consciousness next found me about seven a.m. The room was dark, with the exception of slender lines of sunlight showing around the edges of the heavy drapes and the red numbers on the alarm clock.

"Rick?" For some reason, I couldn't do more than whisper his name. With a whiny groan, I pulled myself into a sitting position and rubbed my eyes. "Rick . . ." It was then that the sound of running water hit my ears. He was in the shower, and I needed to pee.

*Great.*

Making my way across the dark room, I rapped on the door, but got no answer except Rick's warbled rendition of Zeppelin's *Stairway to Heaven,* so I pushed the barrier open. The tiny space was thick with steam, and I felt better just stepping into it.

"Rick," I said louder than before, cutting off his singing. "Don't want to startle you, I just need to use the potty and then I'll be out of here."

He stuck his head around the end of the curtain and I halted the removal of my jeans. Our eyes met, holding for several seconds before I looked down toward the floor. With shuffled movements, I pushed my jeans down and then sat while doing my best to keep myself covered.

"Angel face, why don't you join me in here? The hot water is amazing, and I'm sure you'd love the massage setting."

Looking up, I saw nothing but genuine concern in his azure eyes, so I nodded. He grinned and disappeared back behind the curtain, giving me privacy to finish my business. I went ahead pushing the jeans, and then my panties, to the floor before moving to the sink to rinse my hands so I could rub my teeth with my forefinger. It was a good thing the hotel had the sample size freebies since we'd left our toiletries back at the house in our rush to leave. When it was time to pull my top and bra off, I stilled, nerves overtaking me. A couple of years had passed since he'd last seen me bare, and I knew I'd put on weight.

"Ya coming, Raine?" Rick's voice left me no choice.

I yanked the articles of clothing off and pulled back the curtain with false bravado. By the gentle smile he gave me before stepping back to make room for me, it was obvious that I wasn't controlling my shaking as well as I'd thought. He extended his hand and helped me in.

The shower proceeded with murmurs of "Please pass the soap" and "Thanks." I had to let out a deep breath, and told myself I was being ridiculous when I tensed, yet again, just because Rick started to wash my back. Sensing my discomfort I guessed, Rick started rehashing the previous night, making idle chatter while his hands worked.

"So, from what the firemen were saying, there didn't seem to be any direct cause."

"Oh? But that fire was huge. Are they saying it just spontaneously started?" His hands came around my waist and latched in front of my belly. It was easier than I thought to lean back into his chest; it was comforting.

"No, they're saying it's been a dry summer, and the electrical storm that moved through last night must have resulted in lightning igniting some of the dry moss. That's why we heard that loud pop just before it started. With the moss on fire, it wasn't a far stretch for the old drywall and boards we'd stacked up out there to catch, too. Best explanation they have anyways."

My body stiffened at the words, and he pulled away so he could spin me in his arms.

"Lorraine, what's going on? You looked like you'd seen a ghost when we found those cigarettes. Is there something you're not telling me?"

A deep sigh escaped me. "Funny you should say that, because, um, I think I have—seen a ghost that is."

The moment the words were out, I clenched my eyes shut not wanting to see the look I knew he had to be giving me. The one that would say Rick thought I'd lost my mind. When he didn't say anything or make any move to pull away, I risked peeking out from one eye. He was giving me a look all right, but not the way I'd expected. This was the look that had resulted in three children. I opened the other eye.

"Are you going to call me crazy?" My whisper was thick and heavy like the steam that surrounded us.

Rick shook his head in the negative, and when he leaned in, more than just his lips pressed into me. I soon melted into the embrace, giving in to his long overdue attentions when my body ignited with desire. Fumbling our way out of the shower and into the main room, our clean, wet bodies hit the cold sheets while we kissed in desperation.

Crying out in shock from the abrupt cold on my skin, I tore my mouth from Rick's for a moment, but he rushed to recapture my lips and swallow the sound. His mouth moved over mine, and then with mine once I was able to catch up and return the action. Slow and tentative to begin, together we built the heat between us with cautious movements. We had a couple of hours before we were expected anywhere, so it was easy to give over to the reacquainting.

Knowing that Rick had been vigilant with his gym trips was so different from getting to experience his efforts firsthand. In awe, and with reverence, I let my fingertips discover his defined pectoral muscles, biceps, and strong back while he did the same to me. Welcoming his warm weight atop me, we figured out that the emotional distance had not squelched our intimate knowledge of one another.

Making love to my husband, my partner of over thirty years, was natural. Like riding a bike that had become a bit rusty, we simply had to clean off the dust, oil the chain, and get back on.

"Tell me about this ghost."

We were seated at a corner table in the back at Momma Faye's, after a second shower. Samuel was expecting us to pick him up and we'd decided to come over early to get some food in us before we started the hardest part of the day.

"There's not a whole lot to tell. I thought I saw someone outside a couple of times, and things have been moved." I lowered my voice on the last part. "Oh, and I keep getting bouts of dizziness for some reason."

"Here y'all go. Oatmeal with fresh berries for the gentleman," Dixie winked at Rick, "and for the lady, a short stack of multigrain pancakes; no butter, and honey instead of syrup. Anything else I can get ya?"

"That should do it. Thanks, Dixie." My reply was half-hearted as I looked at the dry, bland breakfast before me, but I'd told Rick this morning I would try to be more health conscious in my food choices. Not verbalized was the commitment to myself to quit smoking. Rick's amused laughter made me look up.

"You'd think you had just been served a bowl of slugs, Raine," he teased, causing me to huff.

"It's not going to taste as good as the French toast and bacon I had yesterday, that's for sure," I quipped at him just before I put a honey dipped bite into my mouth. *Whoa.* "Or maybe it is. Oh, my goodness." I cut off another bite, dipped it, and inserted it. "This is better than I thought it would be," I mumbled with my mouth full.

The deep rumble of his laughter drew my gaze upward. A sparkle I hadn't seen in years was back in Rick's eyes, and I found myself blushing under the look he was laying upon me.

"I've missed you, Raine. I didn't even realize it until all this craziness happened. For that, I apologize."

A part of me wanted to wave off his

sentiments and tell him it didn't matter, but it did matter. I'd been alone the last few years because of his emotional neglect, and to ignore his acknowledgement of that fact would be blasphemous. "I've missed you, too, Rick. So much."

Our hands had just linked on top of the table when we heard a familiar voice. "Mornin' Morrisseys," Samuel chirped while helping himself to a chair and clanking a plate laden with peach pie onto the table. I was beginning to think he didn't eat anything else.

With a quick squeeze, Rick released my fingers and our hands slid apart, but a part of the hole in my heart had been mended; it was a start. We both turned to Samuel with relaxed smiles.

# Chapter 5

## New Friends

The three of us chatted while we finished up our respective breakfasts. Dixie made sure our coffee cups stayed full, and when we were ready to head back to the property to assess the damage from last night, Faye refused to let us pay. What's more, several of the patrons followed us out to the parking lot.

"Rick, what's going on? Why are they all looking at us like they're expecting something from us?"

"Not sure, Raine." His face looked as confused as I felt.

At that moment, Faye came up with a large picnic basket hooked on each of her arms. "These should keep the hungries at bay for the troops until y'all come back 'round for supper this evenin'." Her smile was wide and heartfelt, displaying teeth as white as Samuel's. I had to scold myself for thinking they'd have bad teeth just because they lived in a small town.

Rick stepped forward to relieve Faye of her load with a quick, "Thanks," taking it to the car while she directed her attention to me. Her coarse white hair was escaping from the edge of the handkerchief wrapped about her head, and though her ebony skin was wrinkled with age, her brown eyes betrayed a young vibrant soul. I smiled at her. "Troops?"

"Rightly so, Miss Raine. Most of the town knows 'bout the fire. Word spreads quick round here. It was decided they were gonna come help with that flip o' yers."

"I — oh my goodness, I don't know what to say."

"A simple thanks and a smile is all that's needed. Now, ya best be gettin'. Samuel's sissy will take ya over to Port Royal or Beaufort to check some of the larger home stores while the menfolk do the hard labor." At her words, a slim, quiet girl in a vibrant yellow blouse stepped up. "This here's my daughter, Fiona. Fiona, this is Miss Lorraine Morrissey."

"So nice to meet you, Fiona." The words were genuine as I extended my hand to shake her timid one. The generosity of these people made my head spin.

"Likewise, Miss Lorraine, it's a pleasure to meet you as well." At the shocked look on my face, her full lips curved into a beautiful smile and a soft laugh tinkled from between them.

"My girl's a student up at Columbia, she just happens to be home this week," Faye announced with pride. "She's gonna get outta this town and do great things."

"That's wonderful, Faye. You must be very proud. I can remember how we felt when Lily and Ricky went off to school and their brother Lucas went into the military."

Faye nodded, and her daughter's smile grew wider. Fiona was a stunning young woman: statuesque, strong bone structure in her cheeks, braided waist-length dark hair that showed hints of a rusty color in the sunlight, and of course, amazing teeth.

"Do you have a list of things you need to get?"

"Oh boy, do I have a list!" My laugh was boisterous as I thought of the pages in my purse. With a quick kiss to Rick and a wave to Samuel, we were off, having promised Faye we'd be back about six for supper.

There was about an hour to go until we were expected back at the café when I pulled onto the drive that led up to the house. Fiona and I had hit it off great; the trunk full of assorted shopping bags was a testament to the fun we'd had. I'd even found an adorable bedroom suite, which was being held until I called to set up delivery, from a consignment store in Port Royal. A quick search on my phone had confirmed what I thought: it was hand carved from the local cypress trees, making it a steal at $750.00 for the whole set.

The morning fog had long since evaporated and the heat of midday had faded as early evening set in. It was my favorite time of day: the time when the air wasn't quite so moist, the temperature was bearable, and one tended to get their second wind.

"Let's leave the bags for now and see what's been done. Might be that I just take it all back over to the motel until we get more of the remodel done."

Fiona smiled in answer when we exited the car. As we neared the house, a sensation of being watched crept over me and I became chilled. My eyes darted around, searching out the trees, but it was inevitable that they landed where I'd first seen the fictitious yellow house. Somehow, I kept the groan that escaped me low and to myself when I saw the structure yet again. *Why was this happening?*

"Miss Raine, are you okay?" When I turned toward Fiona's voice, a queasy feeling rolled through my stomach just before a sharp pain overtook my head and everything went fuzzy to the sound of Fiona screaming for help.

The fast approaching ground disappeared, replaced by an old, worn, wooden floor. I shook my head to try and clear it of the cobweb fuzziness I felt. Raising my hands in front of me, I didn't recognize them. They were dark brown, dry, and the skin was cracked in places. They didn't feel connected to my body either. My words got stuck in my throat when I tried to ask what was going on. Swallowing to clear the blockage, I surveyed the room. Before me burned a dwindling fire inside an old-fashioned stone hearth, and to my right, old shuttered windows were thrown open, letting the cooling night air in.

"Girl!"

The hoarse male voice startled me. I spun

around, becoming aware of heavy skirts tangling in my legs.

"Yes, sir." The voice, thick with a low country accent, wasn't mine either, but the sound had passed through my lips.

*What the . . .*

"How many sacks of cotton did you pick today?"

A tremor settled into my arms as panic tightened my chest. Tall and wide, the white man advanced on me. I skittered back toward the hearth at the look of hatred on his face. "None, sir. I's sorry, but my momma —"

"There are no excuses, Jesse. Rain or shine, y'alls task is at least two sacks a day while the cotton's a blooming."

"Yes, sir."

"Did your momma get her two sacks picked?"

Beyond my control, my head shook side to side, and I curled in on myself more while taking another subtle step back. Warning sirens were going off, but it was obvious, I had no say over my faculties, nor did I have any idea what was going on. "She's got the sick, sir."

In slow motion, his hand rose, and I took in every detail: thinning, greasy brown hair slicked back from a shiny forehead, a narrow beak of a nose stretched down the length of his long face to a thin pair of pale pursed lips. His green eyes were bloodshot with the drink that wafted from his mouth. The yellowing linen shirt he wore was opened down to his midchest, exposing pale, untoned flesh. Proof that he relied on others to get the work done.

"*'She's got the sick, sir,'*" he sing-songed, mocking me. "Not my problem, girl. What is my problem is that you owe me four sacks' worth of cotton, and have nothing to pay with."

At his words, an uneasy feeling settled in my stomach. I didn't like where this was going and took another step back, bringing me a little closer to the fire and the iron tools I could see in my peripheral vision.

"But I can think of another way that you can start paying up."

When he came at me, I spun to grab the poker. Before I could reach the tool, arms enveloped me from behind, yanking me back until I collided with a hard chest.

⇜⇝

"Raine, angel face, can you hear me?"

My eyes flew open, and I bolted back. The sudden movement triggered a wave of nausea that couldn't be fought, and I dropped to my knees to retch up the contents of my stomach. A hand pressed against the middle of my back.

"Lorraine?"

Drawing the back of my hand across my mouth, I managed to focus on Rick's face in front of mine. His concerned gaze danced across my face, searching.

"We've got to help Jesse; that man is going to do terrible things to that young girl —"

"Raine, what are you going on about? What

258

man, and who is Jesse?"

"Excuse me, did you say Jesse?" Fiona's wide-eyed visage appeared in my line of sight.

I nodded.

"Jesse Hughes?" That came from Samuel, who had joined us, too.

"I don't know. There was a sharp pain in my head, and then I was somewhere else —" Fiona gasped, cutting me off. I whipped my head around to look at her. *Mistake.* A vengeful throbbing claimed my skull.

She was reaching her hand toward Samuel while keeping an eye on me, and then pulling him into her side, and away from me, while mumbling.

It was hard to tell for sure, but I think she said something about voodoo.

# Chapter 6

## Whispers and Rumors

*One month later . . .*

If you asked me to describe how the last month had been, one word would sum it up: weird. I'd taken to doing what I could with the flip *away* from the house. Ever since my collapse, if I went near the house, the headache, nausea, and chills encroached. I would see things: flashes of the living room and that man doing unspeakable acts upon the girl I now knew to be Jesse. Terror would grip me until my breathing was nothing more than pants and gasps, and lasted until Rick could get me to the end of the drive, far from the house.

Suffice it to say, I was relegated to watching my remodel suggestions happening from afar, through evening pictorial updates on Rick's phone. We'd share supper at Faye's, or sometimes, she'd have po' boys made up. We'd take the sandwiches back to the motel to eat, and then go for an evening stroll along the beach. Considering I couldn't be on the property without having one of the episodes, it was a given that sleeping there was out of the question. At least until we could figure out what Jesse wanted, and how to put her to rest.

The upside to all of this was that Rick and I were finding what we'd once had. Lazy nights in each other's arms helped us rediscover each other in a physical sense, while our beach walks would find us chatting about assorted things to help reclaim that mental connection. We'd talk about the kids if one of them had called me that day, or share anecdotes. Rick's were often pertaining to Samuel's antics, while mine leaned toward what my research at the library had revealed. To be honest, I wasn't digging up much.

According to tax records, Jeremy Hughes was a single man who had been the owner of the property in the late 1700's. While most plantation owners had purchased multiple slaves to tend their fields of long-staple cotton, there was but a single purchase on file for Hughes. The sale consisted of five females: Patricia, her sister Phyllis, and Phyllis' daughters Jesse, Josephine, and Jasmine. No last names, ages, or any other information was given other than that they were bought at the docks in Charleston from the captain of the French slave ship named La Marie-Séraphique in 1770. I couldn't find any information on the girls' father and had to assume he was either left behind in Saint Dominique or killed in the slave round up. It wasn't too surprising that the little knowledge I'd gained managed to lead to more questions.

While my feelings had been hurt by Fiona's kneejerk reaction, she'd apologized after getting a handle on what was happening through Faye's calming words. Now that she'd gone back to school, I missed her. Samuel's take on the situation was the opposite: he was filled with excitement at the prospect of a ghost hunt. As for Rick, well, if he hadn't seen 'things' with his own eyes, he would've had a hard time believing all the talk that had become prevalent wherever we went.

With the passing days, I continued looking into the Hughes' family history, in addition to the property history, while the small bungalow was reborn, and sooner than expected, the house was no longer recognizable as the depressing abode we'd first walked into.

All new plumbing went into the kitchen and bath in addition to drywall and sheetrock. Mid-line appliances kitted out the kitchen so more could be spent on the glass front cupboards, which allowed the space to look more open and spacious than it was. We went with whitewashed woodwork, again in an effort to lighten and brighten the meager square footage. A deep apron sink, along with a mosaic backsplash, finished off the quaint space; the backsplash was fashioned from shattered pottery Faye donated from the café, seeing as at least one dish a day got broken.

Meanwhile, quality fixtures went into the bathroom, except for the tub. I didn't back down on the claw foot staying. To add color, the walls were painted a warm goldenrod, and for a whimsical touch, the outside of the tub was refinished with a merlot glaze before a white and merlot shower curtain had been added. Mirrors placed in strategic locations expanded the space, and a free-standing linen shelf was practical as well as appealing to the eye.

Terracotta tiles replaced the outdated linoleum in both the kitchen and bath. In the bedroom and front area, gorgeous hardwood was discovered when the dank, moldy carpet had been pulled up. A few days were spent stripping and refinishing the planks to bring the wood back to its glory days. Those scary, single bulb light plates were covered up with tasteful light fixtures and the goldenrod paint was used in the rest of the house.

To say I was disappointed when I couldn't be there for the delivery of the cypress bedroom suite would be putting it lightly. In the pictures, it was a perfect fit and added authenticity to the house. Missing that part of the remodel had also been like the straw that broke the camel's back. I was tired of staying away because of a ghost. Life still coursed through me, and I'd be damned if a presence from beyond was going to keep me at bay any longer.

Unsure what to do about Jesse, I'd gone to Faye to ask her advice on the situation I'd found myself in. She'd heard stories of Hughes, and filled me in with what the library source materials couldn't.

According to the local tales, Patricia and

Phyllis had been Vodun high priestesses — the queen mother also assumed left behind in Saint Dominique — and chances were great that they had passed on their skills and beliefs to their girls in secret. Jesse, as the oldest daughter, would've had the strongest bond with Phyllis, and been next in line to become high priestess — perhaps even a new queen mother — had they been able to practice as an active clan. Hughes pretty much kept to himself, and it was on rare occasions that the women were seen in town.

The plantation became the property of the bank after a fire burned the main house and the outlying slave house to the ground in 1772. Hughes' remains were found by what still stood of the fireplace, and it'd been assumed that he'd fallen asleep there with the fire going, an errant coal or embers setting the wood floor alight. An official headcount of the women was never made. The fire was presumed to have also burned them in their sleep when it caught the outbuilding before reaching the cotton fields.

For the first hundred years, the bank couldn't find any buyers for the scorched land. With time, the natural habitat grew back, burying all traces of the cotton under moss and trees. In 1875, a young couple took on the property; building a small, but luxurious for the time, one-bedroom home. The same house that Rick and I were in the process of refurbishing.

The rumors of a ghost began soon after the

young couple had taken up residence in their new house. After a year, the downtrodden wife, who'd been unable to conceive a child with her husband, had insisted it was the house and demanded that they move. The couple was never heard from again. A handful of buyers bought, and soon after, sold the land, always with complaints of mischievous spirits making it impossible to live there.

However, no one ever spoke of having had a similar occurrence to mine. I'd referred to the images as visions, or memories, but Faye was pretty sure I'd been experiencing mild possession.

We had no doubts that the Jesse in my visions, or whatever the episodes were, was the same Jesse who had been purchased by one Jeremy Hughes. What we couldn't figure out was why her spirit had singled me out to approach. I couldn't quite bring myself to say I'd been possessed. Why, after all of those years, and the multiple owners the house had seen, was she targeting me? What made me so special?

Jesse also happened to be the reason why Faye had confessed to me that St. Helena had an active Vodun clan, of which she was the current queen mother.

# Chapter 7

## Ritual

The herb laden incense was making my nose itch and the steady beating of drums behind me thrummed in my ears, but Faye had insisted we needed to do this. She wanted to call on the *loa*—spirits—to ask for guidance and counsel.

We sat outside of our house, where the lightning fire had started over a month ago. Though, now, I had my doubts it had been lightning. In preparation for this ceremony, I'd been researching the Vodun, and found that they believed some of the spirits could control nature. If this were true, I wouldn't put it past Jesse to have started that fire.

Faye had loaned me one of her traditional dresses, which I was wearing while sitting cross-legged; it was a gaudy green in my opinion, but far be it for me to complain. She stood before me in a shocking, bright yellow and pink gown. Beside her was a covered hand-woven basket. Something dark was oozing from the bottom of it into the sand. Ignorance was my friend; I didn't want to know what was inside of the basket. Samuel and a handful of the local boys were responsible for the rhythmic drum beats. Rick sat off to the side, outside of the salt circle Faye had drawn around us. Meanwhile, a trio of women dressed similar to me swayed and dipped in a jilted dance around the perimeter.

My palms were sweating as my heart beat out a staccato in my chest. Staked torches flickered, their light moving with the dancing women. The boys began a low chant in a language I didn't recognize. Almost as soon as Faye began speaking, I felt the familiar tingling of my ethereal guest.

"Bondieu! I am but your servant. We seek an audience with you and your *loa*. Our hearts are pure, our souls cleansed of sin." A splatter of cold liquid hit my face as Faye moved toward me, and then back almost too fast to see. The rhythm picked up tempo, and the dancers moved with more exaggeration.

"Bondieu! Accept the life of this sanctified creature; feed upon it so that we may feel your presence."

I gasped when Faye lifted the basket, and my eyes followed it toward the dark sky. Churning clouds rolled in on themselves, bubbling apart to expose crackling lightning. Rain could be smelled on the breeze.

An overwhelming pressure took over my head and chest.

"Bondieu, before you sits Lorraine, daughter of Savannah, who was the daughter of Naomi, daughter of Nancy. We humbly ask you to guide her spirit family to her, to aid her in knowing why Jesse, daughter of Phyllis, won't let her rest."

I watched while she returned the basket to

the ground and then approached me, hands extended.

"Stand, Lorraine. Bow your head before the presence of Bondieu. Know in your heart that everything happens for a reason, there is no coincidence." Her hands clasped around mine with a fierce grip. "Welcome Jesse into you, let her show you your purpose!"

A loud pop sounded in my ears. I felt the wind knocked out of me. Heavy skirts hung from my hips, and I didn't have to look at my hands to know the skin would be dark and field worn, as once again, Jesse was showing me her encounter firsthand.

"Jesse, ya can't stay here. The master will surely beat us all if he ain't got his cotton . . ." The owner of the voice trailed off to bite down on a guard which appeared to be raw cotton wrapped around a stick. A painful wail slipped out the sides of her mouth.

I let my eyes trail down her body until they stopped on her quivering rounded belly. "I ain't leaving ya, Momma," again the sound of the voice coming from my own mouth surprised me, "Auntie Patricia and the girls will get the damn cotton; ya can't birth this baby on yer own!"

"I've done had three babes already, Jesse Maye! If the master finds out I've had this one, he'll take it and kill it for right sure."

"Don't ya be worryin' about that none, ya

hear? We've got it all planned, Momma; now ya just focus on yer breathin' and gettin' this babe into the world, Bondieu willin'."

The room swirled just as Phyllis let out a gut wrenching cry and my body lurched forward to tend her.

When I could focus again, I was looking into the eyes of a newborn: blue as a jaybird, with splotchy pale skin. Turning the naked girl in my arms, I saw the purplish marks across her back and buttocks which confirmed her mother's DNA contribution, but I was confused by how light the baby's skin tone was. There was also an unnerving familiarity, and I was hard pressed to look away from her; didn't want to.

"Will ya tell me now, Momma, before you go with the *loa*? Who be the father of this babe?"

My gaze moved to take in the bloody mess of a woman on the bed. The delivery had not gone well. Phyllis wasn't going to survive the night. I, we — Jesse and me — reached out to take Phyllis' hand in ours.

"It be the master. He's an evil man, Jesse Maye. Tell your auntie that I said she has to get you girls outta here before he spreads his evil on ya."

The babe squawked, and I shushed and cradled her on instinct. Another wave of dizziness, and time jolted forward again.

It was late and three females — who I assumed were Patricia, Josephine, and Jasmine — dragged into the small shack, halting when they spotted me in the corner with the sleeping baby. Jesse and I had covered Phyllis with a linen cloth on the bed.

Nothing was said by anyone. Patricia came and took the babe from me, nodding me away. The girls set about packing their few belongings into a couple of baskets. I watched with amazement as the plan they'd orchestrated unfolded before me. Once they were packed, more baskets were pulled from assorted hidden crevices and opened to display a variety of bones which they scattered around.

In succession, each one came over to me, hugged me, and wished me well. Patricia was last.

"Remember the plan. We will meet again. Bondieu blesses us." She moved to the bedside, and her finger squelched into the coagulated mess on the covers. Whispering, her bloodied thumb brushed over each girl's forehead, saving her own for last.

They walked out of the shack into the dark, and soon disappeared into the cotton fields just as everything went black. Blinking to steady myself, I opened my eyes with caution, unsure where I would be this time.

I was back in the front living room with Jeremy Hughes lunging for me, but this time, the room didn't disappear when the arms came around me. No, this time I endured the pain and fear Jesse succumbed to as Hughes ravaged her through my struggling body. Somewhere in the distance, I caught a faint whiff of incense and heard the drums, but it was brief. Taking control of my body because Jesse needed to block what was happening to her, I called forth a final burst of strength as he was finishing his desecration and pushed him off.

Not losing any momentum, I scrambled to my knees and grabbed at the iron poker whose pronged tip rested in the coals, and then spun around. An irate Hughes was barreling down on me while I raised the glowing, red-hot iron. Surprised by my action, Hughes didn't have time to stop his advance; in fact, he tripped on a loosened floorboard and fell on top of me. The chunk of metal pierced straight through his chest.

Crying, I rolled his limp body off mine and curled into a fetal position to allow myself a few minutes to sob.

"There, child. It'll be okay. You've done well. Ya know the truth; I can rest."

Raising my wet eyes toward the sound of the soft voice, I found Jesse's wispy form standing in the corner, smiling at me.

"But what do I know?"

"Your roots, and your name, child of Fontenot."

The rest of the vision faded while I watched on. Jesse took a couple of torches out from behind the chair she'd been standing by and set them on fire. "Follow me, Raine," she requested while the room turned hazy.

Her voice floated around me, and I rose to do her bidding, observing as she set one torch or the other against any flammable surface in the living room. We moved out the front door, the torch raising high to catch the moss overhead. Blazing flames licked at the base of the yellow shack, hypnotizing me as the scene wavered and vanished.

# *Epilogue*

Five years have passed since that fateful late summer trip to St. Helena, and we've gone back every year. The flip turned out great, but we didn't sell it. The lands, and the house, are staying in the family and being expanded on. Samuel lives there now with his young bride and their twin sons. Rick and I have never been stronger in our relationship, and are waiting for our first grandchild — a girl who will be named Jesse Maye — to be born compliments of Lily and her husband Scott. He's a close friend of Samuel's. We're all convening on the island to welcome the newest priestess into the family next week.

Rick has retired from his position as partner at the law firm, and has been amazing in helping me learn all I can about the Voduns, seeing as I am part of their honorable heritage. We waited until we'd had a good grip on all that was involved before we went to the kids with the news. Ricky and Lucas have been accepting, but distant. Lily, on the other hand, was as enthralled as me and picked up her Vodun studies right alongside me — under Faye's guidance. That's how she met Scott.

To this day, I don't remember what happened during the ceremony after Jesse took me for a walk through the past. According to Rick and Faye, I began seizing at one point, and Faye had to invite Rick into the circle to help anchor me. We assume that happened during the rape of my great aunt, that moment where I heard the drums.

After I'd slept for two days straight, Faye started in on the inquisition of what I'd seen and heard, and together we broke the components down. Adding in her own knowledge, along with multiple trips to the library, we were able to surmise that Maye Fontaine, Faye's grandmother for whom she was named, was in truth, Jesse Maye Fontenot.

We had to extend our research adventures into Charleston to discover that about the time that my great-grandmother was adopted by the Shaw family, a small group of women traveling under the name Fontaine booked passage to New York. Records show they had an infant with them when they arranged the trip, but not when they boarded.

Everything fell into place and made sense after that: my longing to study family trees and different roots, my fascination with the Gullah culture in general, and the fact that it wasn't luck that led us to buy the St. Helena property, but Bondieu's bidding.

And though no more fires or sightings have happened, I still feel Jesse in the air around me every time I visit. Pretty sure we all do.

*The End*

# About the Authors:

# Forbes Arnone

Jennifer Garcia's (aka Forbes Arnone) love of travel began when she traveled to the West Coast to visit her father at the age of three. Her home until she was sixteen was a small coastal town near Boston. She currently resides in Los Angeles with her husband, two sons, and two dogs.

Her lifelong love for reading and writing was put aside for many years while she made her way in the world and nurtured her young family. Even though she is older, and life never seems to settle, she's finding her way while attending college full-time in pursuit of a B.A. in English Literature. She also runs a business, and is still caring for her family. Believing she can do it all, with the help of her family, she worked on her first novel during the late hours of the night while balancing the rest of her life during the day. Her hard work paid off, as her first full-length novel, My Mr. Manny, will be published August 2013.

# M.B. Feeney

M. B. Feeney is an army brat who finally settled down in Birmingham, UK with her other half, two kids and a dog. She's also a student teacher, a doodler and a chocoholic. Writing has been her one true love since she could spell, and publishing is the culmination of her hard work and ambition.

Her works:

Right Click, Love, part of Sugarplum Dreams, Book four of the Candy Collection

# R.E. Hargrave

R.E. Hargrave is a fledgling author who has always been a lover of books and now looks forward to the chance to give something back to the literary community. She lives on the outskirts of Dallas, TX with her husband and three children.

Her works:

Sugar & Spice, part of Sugarplum Dreams, Book Four of the Candy Collection

To Serve is Divine, Book One in The Divine Trilogy